The Main Point

A Porno Filmmaker's Life & Work

The Main Point: A Porno Filmmaker's Life & Work
BOULEVARD *editions*
London 2006

BOULEVARD *editions*
is an imprint of
THE *Erotic* Print Society
Email: eros@eroticprints.org
Web: www.eroticprints.org

ISBN: 1-904989-21-7

Printed and bound in Spain by Bookprint S.L., Barcelona

Cover Image: Bernd Töst, Avignon, 1962

Bruno Phillips

The Main Point

A Porno Filmmaker's Life & Work

Boulevard éditions

EPS

Contents

Bernd Töst – Auteur and Polemicist

Born of Danish-German parentage in 1934, Töst was raised by his mother in bordellos in Paris and London. After an English public school education curtailed by scandal, the young Töst acquired his film grounding in Soho, working for local blue movie producers. At the end of the 1950s he left England for Denmark where he was joined by his teenage half-sister. Together they formed a partnership that produced his first four porn features and took them to America, where Töst was to spend most of the rest of his life. His sister left him and returned to Europe and Töst went on to create and direct four more substantive films. His work often had dark elements. He was fond of saying that he did not make sex films; rather, films about sex. After 1975 his credited directing career ended. His alcohol dependence and the advent of video left him with little to do other than periodic hack work, which he despised. Despite occasional revivals of interest among avant-garde film buffs and the sex industry he effectively disappeared from view until rediscovered by the author.

Extant Work

Essay: *Social Mores, Semiotics and the Behavioural Zeitgeist as Expressed in Pornographic Films* – unpublished article for *Rolling Stone*, June 1998.

Major Films: *Fotze Liebe*, *Schwanz Liebe*, *Arsch Liebe* (1958), *Melanie* (1963), *Fick Alles* (1965), *Super Bitch in the Halls of the Sex Warriors* (1969), *The Absence of Real Desire* (1971), *The Sick Room* (1975).

Introduction

When Bruno Phillips first approached me with the idea of publishing a biography of porn-movie director Bernd Töst, I was dubious. To my shame, I was only vaguely aware of his work then and the little I knew of him seemed to indicate a failed life: he had failed as a serious film director and failed, apparently, as a successful porn-movie director. Failed, even, as a celebrity, evidently dying in impoverished obscurity. In my defence, his life and career have never been fully explored until now. The more I learned about this extraordinary artist, the more intrigued I became; I recognised that here was a true pioneer, prepared to ask awkward and uncompromising questions about sex and humanity through an admittedly unconventional medium – that of 16 mm celluloid.

True – the Töst oeuvre is pornographic in every sense of that hackneyed adjective. Yet his movies have an undeniable ethos, both of film style and quality of directorial vision. This lifts them out of the ordinary and separates them from the herd. If you watch a Töst movie today you may be repelled or you may find it highly arousing. Either way your perceptions will be challenged. I see him as the Peckinpah or Tarantino of the sex movie. He has created moments of power and beauty from narratives that both exploit and celebrate sexuality, and he has done this from a surprisingly proto-feminist perspective.

In 2006, Töst's era may seem aeons away. Yet the successful revival by EPS of erotic literature and photography from the 1960s and 1970s and the affectionate attention paid to the death of Russ Meyer and the recent revival of *Deep Throat* and *Debbie Does Dallas* remind us that the images from that period possess real power. We Woodstock-generation baby-boomers still have something to say about the presentation of concupiscence. Töst never quite made the crossover from the so-called pornographic to the soi-disant 'respectable' erotic. That frontier has always been a vague one and probably led to his exclusion from both forms. What I love about this biographic appraisal is that it asks us all to think again about –well – a lot of things. As did this flawed but talented, innovative and rather endearing figure.

The author reminds us that in the last days of Töst's often fraught career he would hang around the bars and restaurants of LA, frequented by the glitterati, media and film professionals. As the clientele became more cynical and more youthful the question 'Who's he?' would more frequently be asked. The response from those who knew the answer, however well disposed, did nothing to help his declining fortunes. I congratulate the author on this endeavour, and I'm glad to have played a part in resurrecting a minor, but interesting, figure in the history of sexual politics and the art of their communication: here's to you Bernd.

J Maclean

Author's Note

I first came across Bernd Töst in 1979. I had previously – other than my day job – written the occasional erotic caption, verse, commentary, novel, film script. None of it involved much research or knowledge other than one's own imagination; supplemented by what one came across thanks – profoundly – to the liberation from perceived restraints caused by the ability of people to enjoy sex without apparent penalty. Work and hobby became fused as I travelled. After the business meeting in Copenhagen or New York we young men went out 'on the town'. My business – advertising – was once described as 'the most fun you can have with your clothes on'. Well, it sort of was. What we all wanted – and the girls often shared our ambitions in this – was fun with clothes off too.

This is not always possible, feasible or appropriate. So, with clothes on, one might go to see some really crude, rude and on rare occasions quite stylishly sexy things. Sadly, not often in company with girls. In its day, Manhattan's 42nd Street area, as well as showing hard core loops, put on features of considerable fame. *Deep Throat*, *Behind the Green Door*, and later, *Opening Misty Beethoven*, achieved a quasi-legitimate status. So did the scurrilous but crusading, *Screw* magazine, and its cousin *Suck*. On the continent, the honourable tradition of pictures and films of people getting it on was in full flower. Only in the UK was explicit visual sex illicit.

One day in the early 1980s, I was in Frankfurt with a client of my agency who liked to round off an evening's free dinner with a blue movie – as they were called then. We sat in the sweaty auditorium as the usual trail of energetic girls and studs sucked and fucked and squirted – with the odd intervention of pigs and dogs. Then there was an extraordinary sequence: just a couple; some brief foreplay involving kisses, fingers and so forth. They fuck and come. There was something about the film in its quality, which made it different. The audience in these things is usually either too embarrassed or too bored to show reaction. For this little piece of film there was a collective sigh. I don't know the title, but the brief credit hardly noticed at the time mentioned Bernd Töst. Later, when I met him, he couldn't place the film either, but acknowledged he probably did it.

Years afterwards, by coincidence, Töst emerged in my life. I had spoken at a function, and there was something I had said concerning pornography. This rather gnome-like middle-aged man was introduced to me. He was kind about my piece. In our conversation over several whiskies I recalled the particular film and he declared his identity. It was my shame not to have known more about him, but he seemed glad that the small work I had noted had made an impression. Our conversation lasted for over two hours. It was not enough. But in that time I learned enough about Bernd to care how his reputation was judged. He died three years later. I had not quite finished this book, but at least the correspondence in its development – and a few precious days of his company – has wonderfully illuminated the narrative. I am also very glad he died in the knowledge there was some kind of apotheosis to his career. Not that, as he would have – indeed did – say, 'I give a fuck'.

Bruno Phillips

Acknowledgements

Apart from the man himself, who was a stimulating correspondent and telephonic interviewee even when he was evidently dying, the author would like to acknowledge the Estate of Bernd Töst, for making available surviving archive material. Sadly, many documents and original film stock were lost in a fire shortly before Töst's death. For several reasons, not least those of deference to the living, I have generally chosen to draw on rather than directly quote diaries and personal correspondence between Bernd and his family.

If the narrative sometimes appears disjointed it is mostly because that was how the story unfolded. As a result, some revelations, that occur out of their historical sequence require exposition. Equally, some speculations in the Appendices may have been clarified in the preceding text. But a biography does not require the surprises of a detective novel. Rather, it requires interesting and relevant information at the right time.

Equally, I have had no shame about quoting extensively from my exchanges with Bernd and other witnesses to his life. They were their words and why change them? I thank most sincerely Dwight Brimley, his loyal friend of many years and Louis Bates, his executor and almost lifetime mentor. Both contributed greatly to my interpretation of Bernd's character and personal history. Also, gratitude to my publisher, Jamie Maclean, for his wisdom, gentle guidance and good company, and to my editor, Charlotte Webb. Last, very special thanks to my wife Vivien for believing in Bernd and tolerating my obsession with his story.

The book is dedicated to Hedda and Minou. They made Bernd Töst's life possible and bearable.

Acknowledgements are also due to Isabel Tang, author of *A History of Pornography*, Channel 4 Books, and Joy Publications, publishers of *Wet Dreams*, for books that provided helpful insights and aides memoire, as well as background in relation to the industry and the events of the various periods covered. Any interpretations, extrapolations or apparent inferences are entirely this author's own and have no relation to the content or intent of the source books. References to Bernd Töst's acquaintance with or views on any named individuals, or associations with specific institutions should not be relied upon as statements of fact.

Chapter 1
Frisia, Paris & London, 1934 – 1950

The date of Bernd's birth is uncertain. Records of the period are hard to come by in the aftermath of a world war on the north-west margins of continental Europe. Even more so when the parents are a combination of young peasant girl and transient mercenary. Bernd himself was sure it was in early April 1934 and recalled his mother telling him that the date was the 7th. This would certainly coincide with the diary entry that Töst himself takes as indicative of the date of his conception.

There is no more authentic way to describe Töst's conception than to quote the narrative he himself began, but never continued. Whether it was an aborted autobiography or a film scenario – and so much of his work begs these questions – we do not know. Whatever, here is Töst's beginning, translated from the German:

> *'Hedda Leifsen lay in the soft grass of her native North Frisian water meadows. She pulled the skirts of her dirndl frock and its attendant layers of under petticoat further up her thighs. The wind off the German Sea, infused with summer warmth, caressed her body. Aged nineteen she had the yearnings and instinctive understanding, but little of the knowledge that formed both the impulse and the danger for a girl in her era. Sighing, she let her hand drift down toward her groin. Her fingers pushed under the band of the small clothes*

> *most intimately near her person. She closed her eyes and, without having any coherent image associated with the pleasure her hand was about to conjure, surrendered herself to the moment.'*

Apparently, it was at this moment that Jurgen 'Beau' Töst appeared in her life. In Bernd's effects were some short autobiographical notes from which the foregoing extract is taken. Among these was a reference to a diary of his mother's. Now lost, it could have been in German or Danish. Bernd's brief commentary ran: 'Mama had clearly adored my father and the few years they had together were very happy. As a child I was, of course, curious about my father, who had died before my third birthday. To know that he was funny, charming and heroic was enough for me at the time. Only later, when I was a teenager, I wished to know more; but she would just sigh, or even laugh reminiscently, depending on her mood, and repeat, 'He was a fine man, you have him in your blood.' Whenever I asked about his sobriquet, she just smiled and said, 'He was in the Foreign Legion as a young man.'

'Then, after her death,' writes Bernd, 'I found her diary. It was a pretty normal sort of thing for a girl of her age but there was one entry that made me take notice: July 11th 1933. In rather hasty writing she had scrawled, 'Today, he found me. I wasn't embarrassed. His voice was so kind and soothing. I let him uncover me but he did not force me further. Instead he told me I was beautiful and gave me kisses and such pleasure with his mouth and tongue that I almost fainted.' The following day's entry was even hastier: 'Today, I became his. So happy.'

'Of course,' notes Bernd, in the same late 1970s fragment of memoire, 'I was perfectly sophisticated and the meaning was clear. It struck me as romantic and erotic and I was glad for them.'

The author was able to ask Töst personally about these notes. His response was characteristic: 'So if I wrote it, I meant it.' He added: 'Kids hate to think their parents fuck; why is that?'

To find the family histories of either Jurgen Töst or Hedda Leifsen in their Danish or German context has proved beyond the scope of this book. The flux of powers and frontiers, which constituted the late nineteenth- and early twentieth- century European reality for its populace, had led to considerable mobility. Was Hedda Danish or German? The name suggests the former in parentage, but is no guarantee. The North Frisian islands straddle the border.

We have no certificates, records or any other means of testing Töst's account. He freely admits he led too entertaining a life when young and was too self-obsessed to worry his mother about family history. He wrote to me: 'Your questions are just unanswerable. I wish I could help more – it would be kind of interesting. I think maman [he always used the French term] told me her father was killed in the First World War and her mother died of flu shortly after she and Jurgen got married. He, Jurgen, had been a sailor, had joined the German navy in 1918 and then of course with the end of war, no job; so he joined the Foreign Legion. But I think that Legion bit is bullshit. Going to Guernika wasn't that heroic either. God knows why he did. I don't think he got into the fighting. It was just bad luck being there when the bombs hit. This isn't to put him down. Maman adored him and he must have had loads of charm. Plus, he cared enough to marry her. You know, better to be a dead myth than a live ass-hole.'

After her husband's untimely death in Guernika in 1937, Hedda sought refuge with a distant cousin in Paris. The exact connection is not clear. The cousin, if that is what he was, in fact claimed the Polish title of Count Pietrowski. At the time of Hedda's arrival early in 1938 he was seemingly well-placed, with a large apartment in the fashionable 8e quarter, and a flourishing book business in a house off the Boulevard St Michel[1]. Bernd was scarcely four, so his memories of that time are sketchy. Nonetheless, it is the period when his memories begin. In interviews and the anecdotes of friends, he mentioned how thrilled he was by the jollity and bustle of the ménage. 'There was a constant procession of pretty girls and robust men,' he said to *Paris-Match*, on his last visit to Paris in 1978[2]. 'They would all give me kisses or pat my head. Maman was also very happy and she and Uncle Magnus never scolded me and always seemed to be laughing.' His friend Maurice Girodias once remarked: 'He told me that the Boulevard St

---

[1]*Boulevard St Michel:* This would have been quite a good address. Töst either really didn't know much, or chose to pretend so. There is good enough evidence to suggest that there was some kind of *maison close* there, and that this was even linked to a covert intelligence operation perhaps spying on the French. If so, it would explain how Madame Töst got to England so easily.

[2]*Paris-Match:* Bernd's brief citation and quote was in the context of a feature in the magazine, on an artistic and cultural retrospective of the city's 20th century diversity. He said he had no recollection of the matter, or indeed his reason for being in Paris. He said, 'Oh well, Paris is a village. I think there were still people who knew us.' He was however in Europe at the time. In his terms, 'exiled', albeit temporarily.

Michel, where his mother and the Count frequently took him, was wonderful except there were too many closed doors. He didn't like that.' This hint of a darker side is also confirmed by Bernd's vitriolic comment, just before he died, on the celebrated *La Cage au Folles*. 'That movie is for East Coast liberals and poser grannies. The only thing they got right was the owner was a fruit-cake.'

Whether the Count was all he seemed is questionable. Polish histories and the *Almanak de Gotha* list no one who would fit the bill; the name is common enough.

Paris was full of exiles, intellectual refugees – many Russian – with dubious credentials, and the Count would have blended in perfectly well. He also had money.

How and where Hedda had met Magnus is, again, a mystery. Bernd has no recollection of him appearing in their Frisian home. He does, however, have a letter sent by his mother from Esbjerg to a neighbour. From the text it is evident the neighbour has been given charge of little Bernd and that Hedda has been away for several weeks. Esbjerg is a port. Neither the Baltic, nor Germany nor even Poland is very far away. We have no clue as to the purpose of Hedda's visit. All she notes is that she is glad she went there and has nearly accomplished her purpose in going. It is possible she went in some connection with her husband since the letter is dated July 1937 – only a few months after Jurgen Töst's death. Equally feasible is that she encountered Magnus Pietrowski whilst there, formed a liaison with her Count – why and how the cousin story emerged is also opaque – and moved herself and Bernd to her new protector. Louis Bates suggested to me that the cousin cover story was to protect Hedda's reputation and Bernd's young sensibility from scandal or offence. He says that shortly after Magnus left London, and their household, Bernd said sniffily, 'I never thought he was my uncle or maman's cousin. They made too much noise in bed for that.'

I questioned Bernd in a long telephone call, quite early in this project. He had some recall that his mother might have gone away but nothing, as he put it, 'specific and traumatic enough to warrant therapy'. As to whether Magnus might have been met there he was surprisingly uninterested. He guessed it was possible and pointed out that Hedda was a young and attractive woman. 'Why shouldn't she find some guy with money and start life over?' he said. 'Or at least have a nice fuck.' On the Count himself, Bernd was kind, but surprisingly cool. 'He was good to both of us,' he said 'and I have no complaints. I don't know how really in love they were but maman came across as happy. He drifted out of our lives pretty abruptly but again maman was more pissed off about being poor than by him not being there. I guess he was somewhat flaky but we all had a good time so who cares.'

The nature of Count Pietrowski and Hedda Töst's business in Paris was almost certainly associated with sex. The house address, police records and the long memory of a local ancient attest to this. His bookshop – however legitimate some of its contents – sold pornographic art and literature. The house as a whole was undoubtedly some kind of brothel, albeit a high-class one; perhaps a venue for *partouzes* or a *maison close* in the terms of the time. Töst does remember that 'There were lots of pictures on the walls. I think nobody in them had clothes on and they were kind of tangled up together. I thought they were wrestling. The way the young women who visited us were so nice to me meant I grew up liking women a lot.'

By the age of six, Bernd could speak fluent Danish, German

and French. He could also converse intelligently in Polish. Louis Bates, whom it must be noted was Bernd Töst's house master at prep school, told me how impressed he had been by Bernd's facility with languages. 'It was that which pulled him through his academic troubles,' Louis said. Bernd was modest. 'I lost most of it by neglect,' he wrote to me. 'I couldn't order a beer in Polish now.'

Despite one slight brush with the law – a curious morality and public order charge abruptly dismissed by the examining magistrate – life for this short period seemed extremely happy. Bernd had a combination nanny-tutor, whose teaching style was to take him out to the shops and to the park where she flirted with soldiers. 'But,' Bernd said, 'she chatted away to me so I learned a great deal about the hopes, fears and desires of young women.' Asked how much he thought girls of the same age had changed, he replied, 'Only at the margins. Money, TV and freedom have maybe sharpened their ideas. I never gave it much thought. For most of them, it all revolves around sex, money and some idea of a nice life with a trustworthy person.'

When the war started, Hedda Töst was faced with a serious problem. She was officially a German, albeit with Danish papers. She also happened to be living in Paris with a relative of apparent Polish descent. She therefore did the sensible thing and went – as Bernd said in an interview explaining his controversial use of the Union flag – to the only country likely to offer her the refuge of complete indifference, England.

The intriguing thing about Hedda and Bernd's arrival in England is that it was so easy. Britain was locking up almost anyone with a German connection. Hedda had surely not so soon acquired a French passport? Maybe she was travelling under Danish documentation. This too suggests itself as part of her mission to Esbjerg. Whatever, by March 1940 the three of them had become established in a pleasant terraced villa in Chelsea. Quite how Uncle Magnus managed his life and their upkeep is not known. Hedda put it about that Magnus had a liaison function between the Polish royal family and their British counterparts. Louis Bates dismisses this: 'There was no Polish royal family.' File searches and links in official records also draw blanks. All that can be deduced is that the Count and Hedda Töst had helpful friends. In the social column of 15th March 1941 *Daily Express*, there is a photograph of a royal duke and a cabinet minister at a reception in St James' Palace. Among the background figures are noted 'Count Pietrowski and Mme Hedda Töst' of the Free Polish Legation[3].

Bernd was of course not quite six when he arrived in London. It is odd that even in his last years, when he became more forthcoming, he made little reference to, and indeed seemed irritated by, this wartime period, of which he must have some memories. He said to me, in what I think was our sole and very small spat: 'I missed Paris, I missed Regine

---

[3]*Free Polish Legation & Magnus Pietrowski:* This operation and the *soi-disant* Count's involvement are something of a mystery. The royal connection is almost certainly fallacious. The royal family of Poland had ceased to exist with its well-meaning attempt to have an elected monarchy and the subsequent sad history of that ill-fated country. It is just possible that one or other of the handful of 'Princes' in the uppermost echelons of Polish aristocracy may have been involved but no record exists. The publicly recorded base for the Polish contingent in exile was not the FPL – at best a shadowy group. It may be that Töst got this wrong. It may also be that Magnus was being elusive about his real identity and activities.

(his nanny) and the food was disgusting. Magnus was hardly around, the bombs were scary. I think I wanted the Germans to win as quickly as possible.'

Louis Bates was not yet in Bernd's life. This did not come until 1942 when the eight years old Töst was sent to the nearby St Dominic's Preparatory School. Bates told me: 'Only Madame Töst – as she liked to be called – came to the interview. I never met the Count; his uncle as we were told. Rather surprisingly Madame paid the first term's fees in cash. Later on, payments became a little more erratic, but never more than a term late. She once told me it was getting harder to sell the Count's art collection. She said he was very depressed and the Free Poles kept asking him for money. Later, I found out that the pictures were, in fact, erotic ones, smuggled God knows how from Paris.'

Hedda was, without question, a fond mother. Bernd was happy to recall the night-time cuddles and sudden excursions, which were her style of demonstrating her love. 'I felt loved,' he said. Evidently, she chose to incorporate Bernd as much as possible into her own and Magnus' lives, even when this might be thought inappropriate. In other respects the inference is that they were benignly neglectful. Once asked about his early education days Bernd simply said: 'Yeah, I was in and out of all sorts of shitty places. I hated being sent away from maman and the house.' A fellow pupil at one of Bernd's infant schools recalled to the author: 'He was not over-friendly. Once he was sent home because he persisted in trying to lift a teacher's skirt and look up it.' I related this to Bernd in a telephone conversation and he laughed very much. 'I don't recall, but it's likely. I think I was asked out of at least three of those dumps.'

Later, in a letter, he referred to this period and noted: 'They were real stuffy sorts of places. I often refused to speak English and would swear very softly and very graphically at the teachers in whatever language came to mind.'

This picture of a rather erratic early education is confirmed by later evidence. This was not all to do with his behaviour. He had several long bouts of illness. He also lost an eye in a shooting accident, aged seven. Asked what this accident had meant to him he replied, 'First, keep away from ass-holes. Second, if you've only got one eye, use it to see fucking clearly.' Louis Bates – when I met him, a vigorous eighty or more with an enviable memory – has vivid impressions of that time. In a prolonged interview he recounted his first acquaintance with Hedda and her pale, sickly and wounded child, who was at that time wearing a black eyepatch. It made him, Bates recalled, look like some homuncular rake or pirate.

The young schoolmaster was only twenty, fresh from his own education. He was precluded from joining the military because of his own affliction – a withered arm, the result of childhood polio. Hedda made an immediate impression. Still barely thirty, she had an exotic mixture of shyness, coquetry and willpower. Despite wartime exigencies she retained a Parisian flair for dress and deportment, and was seemingly unworried by her situation in an alien culture. Her English too, if uncertain in syntax, was confident and fluent. It must have been from her that Bernd inherited his facility for languages, especially for their idiomatic quality.

Hedda was direct in her requirements. She wanted Bernd to learn to be a good Englishman. She was convinced Germany would lose, on the grounds that their political leaders were either insane or stupid to take on the British Empire. She admitted that her son was difficult, but pointed out how disordered had been his upbringing, and made much of his genius with languages. She felt that this ability to learn had to be an advantage in a country that had only ever acknowledged French as an alternate tongue, and then in a very limited way.

Louis freely admits he had been enchanted by Hedda. The boy scowled at him and turning to his mother said, in German, 'Maman, I don't want to be here, it smells.' Louis Bates replied immediately, in German, 'You must blame the terrible English food: whale meat and swede. I expect Herr Hitler is eating good sausage.' This made Bernd laugh. Later, as they were shown around the school premises and Bernd asked about Louis' arm, some rapprochement was established. This lasted a lifetime. It cannot truly be described as friendship. Yet Louis was the person Bernd turned to when in need. Sometimes years would elapse without contact, but Bernd always seemed to know where to find Louis – though Louis himself says he was never too hard to find. Those contacts and situations might be seen as Bernd's need for a father figure. This was not so. The role of elder brother might be a closer approximation of the relationship. Bernd was once again reticent about a figure close to him in life, during our last conversations. 'Louis was OK. He was a good thing in my life, like maman, but more reliable. Everyone needs a Louis. I think the old cowboy owes me a call.'

The prep school years at St Dominic in wartime Chelsea, in retrospect, strike all the witnesses as slightly surreal. Bad food, air raids, eclectic pupils and strange assortments of teachers, all grafted on to an effectively Victorian ethos of private English education. The headmaster was a superannuated and somewhat alcoholic quondam colonel of Scots descent who had served in the Indian Army education corps. On a good day he was amiable; on a bad one, prone to dispense beatings for small offences.

There were only two houses. One for the boarders – mostly military sons – and one for the 'day bugs' – numbers of exiled children but mostly the scions of London-based professional, political and, again, military parents. Louis was the youngest teacher but, nonetheless, a house master. He presided over his collection of pupils rather as would a prefect. The primary concern was simply to keep reasonable order and impart a little knowledge. He was somewhat surprised to find that Bernd settled in quite happily. That there was a leavening of foreign pupils helped. Bernd's talent for languages made him welcomed by the native owners of those tongues and commanded general respect. This was less for the skill in general, than for the knowledge of bad language he was able to deploy and share. Possibly for the first time, Bernd felt accepted by, and competent among, a peer group in his adopted country. There were the odd early scuffles, it seems, between Bernd – and other exiles – and the military boarders. Bernd rapidly created his own 'no-go' zone by dint of ignorance of the Queensbury Rules. To bite, scratch and kick was not the way these officers' sons conducted their aggressions. Moreover, Bernd's ability with invective also impressed. For this reason he lived his life at St Dominic's with remarkable equanimity. The loss of an eye was nothing at a time of war. On this topic, Louis only discovered the truth somewhat later. According to Hedda, a French officer visiting their house had drunkenly discharged his pistol at a vase. The vase was shattered but young Bernd, at play quietly beneath, had looked up at the sound and received a shard straight into his eye.

Although he would disclaim too much credit, Louis felt that he had been a stabilising influence for Bernd. This became very important toward and at the end of the war. The Hedda–Magnus alliance was under strain financially, possibly personally, and was shortly to sever. Hedda herself began to visit Louis in and out of school hours, ostensibly to plead her case with regard to the fees. There was also another factor.

Louis had become for her, as to some extent he had for her son, a protector and counsellor. Louis does not deny that he loved Hedda. He does deny being 'in love' and is vehement about the irrelevance of sexual attraction in the relationship. This comes over as entirely genuine. Louis had no family to speak of; for whatever reason, Hedda Töst and her son captured his affection. There is no need to speculate further.

Louis Bates turned out to be a very good protector for the precocious Bernd. Apart from his knowledge of bad language, the child was remarkably well informed about sexual matters. He had no inhibitions about advising his fellow pupils and this was the cause of a scandal, which very nearly led to his expulsion. Both his and Louis' account of this aspect of his development tally very well.

From a baby until he was at least five or six, Bernd had been used to bathing with his mother, or with Regine; and sometimes both. Neither woman had inhibitions about nudity, both adored Bernd. In any case this was not abnormal for the times and in such households: nursery, boudoir and bathroom became places of resort for busy but caring mothers and intimate servants; small boys were also, most often, the centre of female households. It was not very British, but then neither was Bernd. He therefore had no inhibitions about either the female or the male body and its differences. That the household was consistently comfortable in these matters is exemplified by the presence of what Bates described as 'a very well executed' copy of Bronzino's *Venus, Cupid, Folly and Time*, which hung in the drawing room above the bookshop.

Bernd wrote, 'I recall being in the bath with maman and Regine. I'd been ill in bed – as usual at that time – and they were being very affectionate. Maman was soaping me and said something about my dick. She used the French diminutive equivalent of "*pizzle*", "*petit queue*". Regine laughed and replied that, "Today it makes only *pi-pi;* when he is grown it will make a woman happy." It meant nothing to me then, though I liked compliments.' A year or two later, in London and about to go to St Dominic's, Bernd received his first formal lesson in sex.

He had come into the drawing room above the bookshop where Hedda and Magnus were together looking at a large book that was open on the escritoire. They greeted him, but hurried from the room on their own affairs. He went to examine the book. It turned out to be a late nineteenth-century helio-gravure illustrated version of Pietro Aretino's sonnets, drawn and engraved to accompany Giulio Romano's famous *Postures.*

On his mother's return, a dialogue took place which, is worth reproducing from Bernd's own account:

'I said to maman, "What are they doing? Why is his *queue* so big? Will he make *pi-pi* into her?"

She replied, "Well, your *queue* and my *connillon* aren't just there to make *pi-pi*, they are there to help men and women make babies."

I said, "Is that what you did with papa? Did it make you happy?"

"Oh yes, very happy. It was lovely to make you and I am very glad you are here."

"So if I do this with someone we will make a baby?"

"Not if you don't want to. It's not always a good idea to make a baby – especially for the woman who has to grow it. So you have to be very sure. But you can still enjoy the things you can see here. Men and women like doing this because it makes them feel happy, so you can do it for fun."

"When can I start?"

"Not yet, little man, you have a lot to learn."'

Bernd simply notes at the end of this piece: 'So I kept asking for more information and she told me and let me look at pictures and read books until I decided I knew enough for the time being.'

Reading was another of Bernd's precocities. He had been reading since three years old. His mother, and later Regine, had enjoyed reading aloud to him. The chosen books were not standard children's fare. They tended toward the romantic bodice-ripper style. As soon as he could read quite well they would let him share the narrative and he became well-versed in taking the male part of villain or hero. This included becoming the cause of the female horror at the advances of the wicked squire, and the recipient of the warm embraces and kisses of the heroine for her saviour. He recalled the frequent ending of a dramatic reading with himself and either of the two women shrieking and giggling as they struggled in his childish embrace.

In the paranoid atmosphere of contemporary Britain

this reads like dangerous stuff. For Bernd it was natural. It was compensation for his shifting world, for his injuries and illnesses. It secured his sense of personal identity and it allowed him to like women. Unsurprisingly, if his knowledge of children's classic literature was deficient, that of adult romantic and physical relations was too far advanced for authority. The practical accounts he gave of how it all worked were soon relayed back to parents by their enthralled sons, respectfully keen to have their schoolfellow's version confirmed. Bates had overheard one 'seminar' and had tried to head crisis off at the pass. Too late; Bernd had provided several pupils with simple sketches of the immediate anatomies. They were apparently rather good, but two or three escaped Louis Bates' attempt at censorship.

Luckily for young Töst, the headmaster was on one of his periodic absentee binges at the time. Bates was delegated to resolve the matter. This he did by means of a grovelling apology, the excuse of necessity in having to cope with the consequences of war, and a promise that there would be no recurrence. Luckily, only one parent withdrew their child immediately, and Bates was serendipitously able to create two new places courtesy of introductions from Count Pietrowski. Bernd was, however, warned that ignorance was the essential quality on these topics, and if pretence of ignorance were repugnant, a plea of enforced reticence would do.

At eleven, through Louis Bates' helpful contacts, he was sent to a reasonably good, if not top drawer, public school in Buckinghamshire. The headmaster's comments on his entrance exam results noted: 'These inspire hope rather than confidence.' Once again, information is sketchy about these early years. School records from the time show him at age sixteen to have been a decent enough athlete. He played for the 2nd XV and rowed for the 2nd IV; the latter with some distinction, winning several cups.

Few people, however, seem to remember him. One contemporary pupil, David Brooke, later Lieutenant-General Brooke, does have a memory. 'Foreign sounding name, but to hear him he was English. Good egg really, not a shirt lifter, or a blubber; gutsy rugger player too. Put him in charge of the junior ticks' dorm after a bit. What did he do later?'

Bernd himself said: 'It wasn't a bad place. Like *If* without the great denouement.' He also hinted at other adventures. In discussing his much debated film *The Sick Room* he responded to a feminist critic: 'You've clearly not come across assistant matrons in boys' boarding schools.'

The school was no more helpful than Bernd in memories or records except for what has been recorded above. It seemed Hedda had forgotten – or avoided – a subscription to the Old Boys' Association, so her son's name never got on the list. This only worries a biographer. Bernd wrote to me: 'Don't be so obsessive. There's nothing to tell. The food was bulky and I learned to love burned sausages and unwashed lettuce with caterpillars – great for table racing – and baked potatoes with cheap margarine. Having wanted the Germans to win the war I did begin to feel sorry for them as losers if this was how the winners lived. That said, I did OK in the ritual fight you must have in the dormitory on your first night as new boy, so the pack accepted me. Curiously, though there was some pretty terrible bullying, it never touched me. Despite a foreign name, which made me 'wog' to everyone, and only one eye, I cruised along, just one of the crowd. Who knows how these things work?'

Back in London, after the war's end, his mother and the Count had fallen on more difficult times. Despite his wartime role – whatever that had been – Magnus could find no work. The change of regime resulting from Russian domination of Eastern Europe made Poland unattractive. However, it seems he was under real pressure to return there, whether from the British or Polish authority is unknown. Louis Bates, who remained in touch with Hedda, believes it was a mixture of both. As an already equivocal refugee and whatever his temporary utility in England, Magnus was now surplus to requirements. Equally, the new myrmidons of the Communist hegemony seemed anxious to retrieve at least some of their strays.

Bernd professes (and it is probably true) that he was in genuine ignorance of exactly how things were at this time. His files have a couple of short letters from Hedda written during the Spring of 1946. Amid the conventional sentiments she observes, 'I fear there will be some changes in our household when you come at the holiday, but do not be alarmed, Herr Professor Bates has arranged matters. All will be well.' Oddly, this letter is in German, though she and Bernd most often used French for their intimacies of expression. Bates was always described as Herr Professor by Hedda.

The conclusion of this uncertainty was that by the end of the year Magnus retreated to Paris[4] and Hedda moved to rented, but comfortable rooms in Meard Street, Soho. This must have been a serious shock at the time for both her and her son. It was mediated for her by some form of financial arrangement that both paid her rent and Bernd's school fees. For Bernd, it created a whole new, exciting and ultimately seminal environment. If we remember his cosmopolitan upbringing and his facility with languages, it is not difficult to see how comfortable he would be, even aged twelve, in the polyglot and louche environment of London's most sinful quartier.

Asked directly, Louis Bates merely twinkles and refreshes his whisky glass. 'Some things,' he says, 'are best kept in the dark.' In that interview with this kindly and engaging man nothing emerged that was admitted or even acknowledged as likely. Nonetheless, the author ventures the following scenarios to explain the Töst household's successful transplant and apotheosis.

First: Magnus is on short notice, but through his contacts is able to negotiate a *laissez-passer* from the country for himself and a *laissez-rester* for Hedda and, of course, Bernd. It may even be that Louis Bates becomes some kind of sponsor for Hedda and/or guardian for Bernd. Wild ideas that he may have married Hedda are simply not confirmed in the marriage certificates of the time.

Second: A combination of Magnus and Hedda in agreement over the division of the assets leaves Hedda with at least something to sell. The contacts of Louis Bates enable fees to be waived or

---

[4]*Return to Paris*: Why Magnus was forced out of the UK and what he did in Paris is unknown. Quite probably he had played both ends against the middle for too long. What is fairly certain is that he went back to Warsaw as an old man after the collapse of the Soviet Union and died at the age of around ninety. Sadly, it seems, he and Töst had not stayed in touch. Even sadder, neither had Minou; and she herself resisted any discussion of her father.

some scholarship to be offered for Bernd's school fees.

Third: However strained their relations, Magnus and Hedda had conceived a child – probably during the late summer of 1945. The records of the Westminster registrar tell us that Melanie Pietrowski was born on 10th April 1946. Her mother declared as Hedda Töst – French refugee; her father as Count Magnus Pietrowski – Polish exile. Louis Bates gave me this information quite late in our acquaintance and in his usual gnomic way, merely inviting me to look in the Westminster registry for the date in question. Possibly the changes Hedda referred to in her surviving letter included a baby. That the little Melanie – or Minou as she became – existed and was Hedda and Magnus' last productive work is not in dispute. How Bernd dealt with the reality of a sudden little sister is another important thread in his story; to which we shall return. It will not escape attention however, that the month and date of their births were virtually coincidental.

Whatever the mixture of forces, there is no doubt that the Töst/Pietrowski partnership retained some serious and tangible assets for collectors. That these had to be deployed to provide a capital base and income is the logical conclusion. The only admission Louis is prepared to make is, 'I sympathised with and liked them (Hedda and Bernd) both. I did what I could.' The inference is that whatever he did, it was more than helpful.

Bernd was perfectly comfortable with the move on his own evidence. Precisely what Hedda felt about her life is harder to discern. Her son admits he had 'become a teenager' and was somewhat self-obsessed. Boarding school had removed him from the cosy female establishment into a harder, more masculine world. His own hormones also drove him toward a less protected future.

'Maman' could manage her own destiny. The Hedda who had not so many years before swooned to the embrace of a passing sailor in a Frisian meadow had long since grown up. She had managed a brothel and an erotic bookshop in Paris, and now maybe London. She had negotiated – albeit with help – a division of assets with a lover of doubtful provenance: all this in foreign countries, and under restrictive moral regimes in uncertain times. To be in Soho in 1946/47 with her competence was to be in a land of some opportunity. Hedda had no great entrepreneurial ambitions; only the desire to provide for herself and her family. The times were not easy, but as a good-looking, clever woman in her thirties she conveyed both sex appeal and authority in a rapidly evolving post-war London that, in Soho at least, welcomed the bohemian, the astute and those likely to possess or generate money. If there was a problem, it must have been that she had to bring a child to term as a single mother. Hedda was, however, a seasoned survivor.

Quite old and wise enough to know what was going on at this time, her son remained politely stalwart in his refusal to speculate or even say much about their life together at this point. That was his prerogative. Piecing together the evidence, it seems most probable that Hedda used her personal skills, contacts from Chelsea and Paris and the chaos of the time to put together something like the network of customers and events that had been the hallmark of the Paris days. In addition, she must have taken some time and trouble to explain the arrival of a baby in their household. This probably would add to Bernd's coolness toward Magnus.

In an [openly] recorded phone call Bernd told me: 'We had this slightly sleazy landlord – Ricky something, Maltese, whatever. Anyway, maman had not only got these rooms from him, but she persuaded him to let her have some deal on the entire house. It was crummy, but it was elegant and late Georgian. So in next to no time, it's like Paris all over again.' At the time of this conversation, early in 2000, at the start of our relationship, the author had no knowledge of Minou. Her appearance in Bernd's life comes later in the narrative.

The move to Soho could not have been better for the teenage Töst. He had an engaging style. He could be warm, funny and very obliging. He could also exude an air of menace, especially when he used his disconcerting stare – even more so without the black patch that later became his trademark – which he referred to as 'blindsiding people'. In short, when at home on holiday, he soon found work in and around the louche milieu of the area. 'Sex, food and booze,' he once remarked. 'What else would any intelligent kid want?'

His permanent arrival in Soho was earlier than he might have expected, or than Hedda hoped. It was occasioned by his expulsion, in 1950, from the public school in which his parent and 'guardian' had invested so much. The 'cause célebrè' – luckily denied celebration by the newsprint restrictions and residual social inhibitions still prevalent at the time – was his apprehension in flagrante aged sixteen with the school assistant matron. An affair, it transpired, that had gone undetected for three years.

'Oh, wow, you bastard!' was his first response to my general summary of the information I had gleaned. He became more assured as I explained and reminded him that he had right of veto, that we had an independent attorney who would ensure nothing could be published without his, Bernd's, approval in writing. 'So back there in the UK, being fucked age thirteen by some sex-crazy chick of twenty a long time ago doesn't get you arrested?' I said, 'No it doesn't, and if it did you can sue me.' Then Bernd told me about his experience; from which he determined that religion and sex were the two opposing forces. His choices were made at that moment. What is now written is what he sent to me – as habitual – on a tape with the sleeve annotated 'use this'.

'So in this weird English school, fucking freezing. It was the winter of 1947. Snow higher than a cow's tits. The other kids hadn't even made it back from the Christmas break. Maman of course had some guy drive me down there in this big Humber, on the due date. It was a crap journey but the driver was good; Christ knows if he ever got home. There was this great lady – Noreen was her name. She may have been about twenty but to me she was a lady. She was the junior matron, that is, the paramedic for all of us spotty pubescent boys. We, the head man and a couple of the resident male teachers were the only people who had got back to deepest rural Buckinghamshire. I was in the dormitory and Noreen comes in and says: "You must be cold, do you want to come into the matron's room?" So I did. How do these things happen? People want too much narrative. We were cold and lonely and why she wanted me is her problem. I thought she was terrific – a boy's dream. Then we have cocoa and some dialogue in this excellent sitting room with armchairs and all the nice stuff that people in charge get for their personal use. She suggests a warm bath would be good.

'Noreen strips off her blouse and skirt, so she is just in brassiere and knickers. To be candid, in those days, bras and knickers were not terrifically exciting. That said, if you're thirteen and even if you were sophisticated like I was; well, girls with underwear suggestive of possible nudity are where it's at. Even now, I can recall how truly crap I thought English female underwear was at that time. Quite possibly it is because most of my acquaintance with girls had been with either nakedness or frilly stuff. Anyway, we are soon naked, and we splash around in a big tub full of hot water. Outside the snow falls and I remember the window freezing up and real cold air drifting through the cracks and Noreen has these great breasts, just right you know, and her nipples are stiff and, well, like girls' nipples are, though it could have been the cold. We, or rather, Noreen, have a short chat about how my dick is up and where did I get such ideas. So we get out and there is lots of stuff with towels and she smells terrific and my dick is rigid. Then it's her mouth around my cock and my first blow job. I will always thank her for that moment. She has no problem with me coming into her mouth. That is, of course, the male fantasy. Semen is an acquired taste, and it doesn't arrive with gastronomic credentials. Believe me, the girls who swallow because they love it are pretty scarce. If they do it, it is because they want to give you a gift and can cope because it isn't that bad; or because they are very submissive, which can be part of how they get off. Anyway, Noreen snuffles and jerks and licks and I shoot it and she sucks it down. "Oh, you bad boy," she says. "How did you get so big, and so virile?" Perhaps she meant it, but it did my ego a lot of good. That moment was the real beginning. My school life centred round fucking Noreen. All the classes, sport stuff, winning cups and so forth was peripheral. It didn't occur to me that I was thirteen or fourteen. I had this terrific girl with bouncy tits and a juicy cunt who loved to fuck with me. How we got away with it for so long is a mystery to me. She really enjoyed my licking her out. Oral sex takes different engineering from a fuck – especially the bend-over quickie at which she and I became adept. All teenage boys, I imagine, have instant erections, so when she gave me the call – time for your injury massage – there was no problem; undress, cock out. But also she loved to be sucked out herself and rightly so; and this needed prep.

'Personally, I quite like a whiff of the jungle, but it's the lady's choice. The spontaneous or explicable meeting in the school sanatorium where we usually had our meetings meant more when I could suck her off. She liked to lower herself over my face. She had very fleshy labia, amid a lot of fur, and her cunt had this fantastic smell, like a great delicatessen. She liked me to drink her juices, shove my tongue into her vagina, lick her ass and generally collect her whole sexual bits as cocktail, hors d'oeuvres, entrée and dessert. I would go to sleep thinking about her cunt and the way her ass cheeks spread. They are fascinating enough in pictures, but in real life, boy, works of art. My dick would be sore, because when I blew her, she'd be pumping and chewing my cock and I'd be hanging on until she came because that was when she'd be least worried where the come went. Mind you, she did like me squirting over her tits or belly. She'd hold my cock and watch quite thoughtfully as if trying to remember. I guess I felt that about her cunt. After she'd come, I'd lie with my head on her thigh and stare into her crotch as the lips closed and the juices congealed and think, oh boy, this is about being alive. You know, writing this has been good. That was three of the best years of my life. It gave me the real-time sex education all boys should get. She never took it up the ass though. I hope she's done all right for herself. There's a good deal of double-dealing out there – especially for risk takers.'

It is not hard to see how his film themes developed from all his early sexual experiences. Not only in the approach to the physical aspect but also in relation to what he saw as the hypocrisy of 'legitimate' film and the shoddiness of the porn business. Whatever we think of Bernd's work, David Wilson, doyen of critics and film historian, once wrote, in a review of Töst's *Super Bitch in the Halls of the Sex Warriors*. 'There are any number of perfectly respectable studios, directors and actors who want to 'do sex' under the guise of artistic legitimacy. I am sure there is also a respectable if not equal number of people in the porn business who would love to get some art into the sex. In this rather thought-provoking film, which, to coin a phrase, puts the girls on top, Töst doesn't quite make the case; but I have to admit, the sex is very well contextualised. Overall, this is an intelligent movie. Sadly, you'll have to visit some weird cinemas to see it.'

Bernd himself was fully aware of this problem. Whatever his childhood had taught him, Soho provided the commercial context for it when at sixteen, his academic career over, he returned to Meard Street full-time in 1950. 'Sure,' he once said, in an interview when asked about his views on films like *The Devil in Miss Jones*, 'that was a brave try. There have been others. Some of the early stuff in the 70s had its heart in the right place, I suppose, looking back; but it was too much just cock-sucking and no sense of drama or where the women were at. In the end it's about the percentage. Video fucked it all up, though I have hopes for digital. The whole fucking consumer market is about lowest denominators. Cost, taste, whatever. Some people say it's all too much. I say it's all not nearly enough. Except highest margin for the distributor. You have to look to the art world. When are big dicks and wet cunts going to be in the galleries? That Turner prize thing is sort of nudging the edges and everyone's going oh, wow, what do we have to think? Well, art has to help out here. Is sex horrible and dirty and secret or is it fun and what we do? There was one movie that did a great job on this called *WR-Mysteries of the Orgasm*. Ran a while in the seventies, buried because no one could deal with it. I get panned because my movies show cunts and mouths and asses with cocks in them. It isn't all they show but that's the main issue. I say, so sure, the cock is dramatic. Where it gets put is also truly interesting. So, I point out that the cunt is even more fascinating and wonderful and enjoyable. I don't think feminists just hate cocks, I think they are embarrassed about their cunts.'

In the journalist's notes after this interview in 1987 he records: "Bernd sat back and laughed and said 'Oh Christ, how do we ever make sense of all this? I mean, why are we so worried about the cock and cunt thing? In my films I've tried to show that it's the one and only, the real, connection. Before, so maybe there's the empathy and the context and the motivation and all that stuff. After, it's how do we deal with it. In the middle it's just the raw 'whoo'eee'. Fact is, babe, it's the raw 'whoo'eee' most people get excited and upset about. But we have to give it decent decor, nice tablecloths, flowers in a vase and a fancy menu to make it at all palatable. Even then most often we decide the decor and the pretend is fine and can we just sniff the prawn cocktail and go home. *La Grande Bouffe* could have been a great movie but they bottled out on the sex thing. I mean, why is it OK to show a guy shitting himself but not with his dick out? Look at *The Postman Always Rings Twice* or almost any publicly certified movie. I include Carrie Fisher in her scene with Jabba the Hutt, which the whole world found mega-erotic. We always run away from expressing the idea of sex and what is really happening here. Sure, in a general movie you can understand but it's all so sneaky. We're so frightened of the bad – it would certainly be gross to have Jabba licking the princess out – that we daren't show the good – here's two film actors enjoying a fuck. Trust me, I know why really, but there is too much hypocrisy in movies."'

Living in the Soho milieu meant Bernd would always be on the borderline between the legal and illegal. It was a line he managed to walk quite skilfully. In his own account he dismisses any idea of cleverness. He observed to his friend Lasse Braun – himself successful and well connected: 'We were all in the same village trying to earn a living, the cops included. Do your work, be a nice guy not a wise guy, and, above all, keep your mouth shut.' Lasse apparently replied: 'Nice came a long way down the list.'

He has also been quoted as saying: 'Bernd was keen and smart. He was impatient with the constraints of the British porn business. When I first met him he was already an editor – this was before video. He told me that the producers of the films he worked on were cheap bastards and the directors were talentless cowards. It was his opinion.'

All this was in the future. By 1950, the household in

Meard Street had evolved. Hedda had made a real success of her enterprise. The 'club', although licensed to a third party nominee of her landlord [his accountant], was effectively hers. 'Hedda's place' became an essential point of rest for an eclectic if dissolute group of theatre, political and film people. In its hey-day, it rivalled 'Muriel's' in Greek Street in the Soho kultur as a venue. Hedda's was the more commercial, and catered for the moneyed and 'managerial'. It gave the chance of meeting pretty, fun but also intelligent girls, with the enjoyment of 'diversions' in the various private rooms on upper floors or elsewhere. Everything was very discreet and it is to be assumed that, despite a continuingly censorious post-war London, the police were comfortable with the club and appropriately convinced by Hedda's protector and business partner.

She presided over this establishment with flair and charm. A British Member of Parliament of that era wrote in his autobiography: 'I got away to Meard Street, thank God, after a dreadful evening in the House. The lovely Hedda was of course there and dispensed comfort and happiness as ever. I wished she could run the Commons and told her so. She laughed and said, "Oh Mr Charles, how would we have any fun?"'

Also, in Greek Street was a hostel for young female actresses. Strictly controlled, it had the very proper aim of offering a secure environment. But not every resident wanted to earn a living between parts by working as a shop girl. Judiciously, Hedda offered suitable candidates the opportunity to meet and enjoy the company of influential and affluent men. The consequences were mixed; several divorces offset by a few marriages.

Whilst she retained a practical and cordial relationship with other professional ladies in Soho, Hedda was meticulous in her construction of the appropriate 'Chinese walls', so that she could assist the more impetuous of her customers without risk. Soho was full of girls, both professional and casual, but discretion was everything to Hedda's business. As she told Bernd when he arrived home following his expulsion, 'My darling boy, remember only that in this house, even if St Michael and the angels raided us, they would see nothing but pleasant people enjoying each other's company.'

Hedda's love for Bernd apart, the arrival of an adult male in her household would have been very useful. He was young certainly, but Bernd was rather older than his years, and his cosmopolitan upbringing, coupled with his very strong affections for his mother, made him a good watchdog. In addition there was Minou. At four years of age she took increasing amounts of Hedda's attention. As for Bernd in Paris, there were always pretty girls to be nice to the child, but finances did not run to a Regine. For both the Töst females, Bernd's return was very pleasing. When ultimately, and very shortly before his death, Bernd was willing to talk about Minou with me, he said: 'Yes, she was always a total cutie. When maman told me I was pretty pissed off – not by having a sister, but because Magnus had gone. Maman was damn stoical about the pregnancy and she had the kid and so I had a sister. Being away at school meant I didn't have to go through the baby stuff too much. I think Louis was pretty heroic at that time, though I didn't really appreciate it. Anyway, there's your own life and then you get back and the baby is talking and it grabs your hand and next thing you're doing incy-wincy spider and other stuff like bathing the kid and walking it.'

It is easy to forget how difficult life was at that time in London. There was rationing, smog – that lethal amalgam of smoke and fog – and the rebirth of international tensions in relation to Berlin. There was no central heating, but lots of coal and gas lamps still. As everyone from that generation recalls, life was lived in grainy black and white. There was also a vivid camaraderie of local life; circumscribed but able to be circumvented. Bernd told me that the only thought he had about the Berlin airlift was he wished they would have one to London. Fortunately in Soho, and in the centre of London, there were usually means of obtaining things – clothes, food especially – not readily available elsewhere. So the sixteen-year-old Töst was busy being his mother's aide-de-camp, finding work and being a good elder brother to Minou.

Chapter 2
Soho, First Breaks & Minou, 1950 - 1962

Louis Bates, as ever, gave me the first insights on the evolution of Bernd's relationship with his sister. Hedda had been very anxious about how to tell her son that Magnus' parting gift was a baby. Deferred as long as possible, the evidence and its admission had become inescapable. So Hedda sent Louis down to Bernd's school.

In the Spring of 1946 he took the train to Amersham on one of the traditional 'leave-out' Sundays when boys could go home or be visited and given treats by parents. The times were not conducive to much use of this opportunity and Bernd, like his school-fellows, regarded these Sundays as a break from the routine of worship, meal and study. The usual activities were cycle rides into the country. Hedda had never been a great visitor and later, Bernd preferred his trysts with Noreen. As he observed more than once: 'The only time I believed in a God was then. Some angel must have protected us from discovery.'

On the Sunday in question, Louis announced himself by telegram. He recalled that it simply declared his arrival and added something to the effect of family business but not to worry. He says that the initial conversation was in the school grounds, walking around the playing fields. There were no short cuts and no attempts at circumlocution. Louis rightly felt directness was the only way and so simply said: 'I am here because your dear mother wishes you to know you are to have a sibling. The father is, of course, Count Magnus.' Bernd's initial reaction was indeed to be 'pissed off' and to blame Magnus. There was a passage of stamping around and swearing and use of epithets; then, a few tears. The emotional well-spring can only be deduced. Possibly the jealousy of an only and cherished child, maybe a sense his beloved 'maman' had deceived him; even anger that his 'uncle' had not merely left them, but added to their problems. It should also be remembered that Bernd was still rather new to the school and had yet to discover Noreen as a diversion.

After the emotional catharsis, in which Louis says he said little except, 'Your maman and little brother or sister will need you. You are the man of the family,' they went for luncheon at a nearby hotel. Louis says that apart from the food being as expected for the times, all went well. Bernd cheered up and started asking questions about when the baby was due and so forth. After which he lost interest and they talked about London and school and Louis admits he let Bernd covertly share his claret. Töst himself, when he finally began to tell me about Minou, confirms this résumé of that encounter. 'Pretty much it,' he scrawled on the fax I sent with these and other paragraphs – he never took to email. Later he would say much more, and it is evident that, from her birth, Bernd took a lively and affectionate interest in his unexpected little sister.

In the short period of, as it were, his puberty, his apotheosis as functioning sexual male and male family protector, Bernd had what must have been a rather surreal, multiple existence. As boarding schoolboy, he had to bow to the regimes and perceived wisdom of the culture. English 'public' schools had their own imperatives and style, regardless of their relative status in the hierarchy of such institutions. Within that 'kultur' he had achieved a level of subversion. Much is made of the homosexual element of English single sex education. Bernd and Louis both agreed when we – separately – discussed these matters that this has been grossly overrated. Much of the time, discreet – or even not so discreet – masturbation was the solution, ideally accompanied by some kind of visually aided fantasy female as permitted at the time. Louis Bates was kind enough, on behalf of the boys, to thank *Draper's Record* for its pleasing advertisements for underwear. Of course there were boys who needed to deal with the simple physical and mental demands of sexuality in puberty in what might be called a 'social context'. This satisfied most of the 'experimentation' criteria. In effect, the result was most likely to be social or mutual masturbation. Beyond this lay what, for most, was an unknown territory. As Louis confessed – and this is a precis – all British public school boys know that the idea of 'prettiness' starts with slim pre-pubescents. Some are 'pretty', some are not. In the era when classics were still taught and sometimes understood, we all knew the Greeks had a word for it. Whatever it was, and however pretty the occasional junior person happened to be, even if in the libido they were fuckable, boys knew it was about girls. Those who did not kept quiet. The real sanctions were to do with what is nowadays called abuse. Louis said, 'Bernd and I talked about this when we had our lunch. He told me that there had been a master in the school who had tried to seduce boys and he had been mocked out of the place. He also said that the 'prefect' who ran his House, was adamant about ensuring that anyone who was keen on young boys was identified. There was an understanding of the difference between juvenile experiment and adult predilection.'

Imagine then, a young man, informed beyond his years, although – for the moment – still a relative ingénue in life experience, having to return to Soho in periodic visits with a slightly distracted mother and now a baby sister.

The birth in the Frith Street Women's Hospital occurred without witnesses and during term-time. It was easy enough, and with some trusted staff from Meard Street going to and fro, Hedda was able to stay for the then usual ten days of post-natal nursing. Louis undertook the registration. Bernd arrived a few weeks after, when Minou was home and in her cot. From the accounts of Louis and the few other witnesses to the time, Bernd was a good older brother. He himself was happy to say that he fell under the spell of this little girl. Maybe too, in her eyes he saw those of his mother.

Of this time preceding Bernd's expulsion from school, there is little witness, and neither Louis nor Bernd is willing or able to add much. All of us have periods in our history when the 'nothing much happened' caveat applies. Even so, whatever the distractions of Noreen at school, in Soho, during the holidays, Bernd was trying to be a brother-father-husband-partner figure to his mother and Minou. This in addition to his personal ideas about how he wanted to express his own demands on life.

Louis Bates says that Bernd did very well. He told me that Bernd spent a lot of time with Minou, in the early days when he was at home. He would talk to her, give her a bottle if Hedda couldn't do so, even change her nappy. The child quickly became habituated to Bernd – despite long absences whilst he was at school – and Louis remembers her asking, 'Where BeeBee?'. This became her nickname for Bernd. No one could recall how little Melanie became Minou.

Part of the process by which – from my first introduction to Bernd, Louis and the history – one can measure how we went from suspicion to trust was how we dealt with Minou. That she was cherished was not in dispute. Bernd assumed the role, not just of male in the family, but in some contexts, mother. The early dialogues, when we had come to terms with what it meant to collaborate in a biography, were necessarily reserved. The revelations emerged slowly. Minou became the test of our trust in each other.

If we decide that Bernd has become not just Minou's elder brother but also her father/mother, we get into complicated waters. The author's own view is simply that Bernd was quite secure enough to welcome his sister and fit her into his own life ideas and the practical situation. Even more, he took on the male role of protector for the enhanced female household. This is not to suggest that Bernd saw himself that way. Rather, that there was a specific job to be done – to support his mother – and that his adoption, emotionally as well as practically, of Minou was a means by which he could demonstrate his love for Hedda. She reciprocated; Bernd was central to her life. She seems to have been more equivocal about Minou. In any case the management of her business took up a great deal of her time and energies.

'You people are too smart for me,' Bernd said, when I was reviewing the text of this book with him. 'If that's your take, so be it. These were just the people in my life I cared for.' However considered, the reality is that Bernd and his little sister became close companions, friends and allies for eighteen years.

Help with Minou's upbringing apart, Bernd had to take his place in the management of the Töst household economy. Whilst things were getting a little easier for the general population and rationing was near its end, the overall standard of living was poor. Bernd had to learn fast about the intricate network of contacts, favours exchanged, obligations and useful skills that helped the quality of life and made Soho work. One of his contemporaries recalls, 'He was a busy kid. He was always about, doing things: messages, deliveries, looking out for people's stalls or shops if they needed time off. He quite often had this baby with him; we liked that, it made him genuine. It was also very good cover. You know, in case. I didn't know him that well, but he was reliable and did me some favours too.'

Part of Bernd's role was to arrange some of the entertainment at Hedda's, in the private rooms or elsewhere as appropriate. As a club, they had some latitude in terms of licensing and censorship and it is in acquiring the films that Bernd gained his first experiences of the British blue movie business.

Provision of any form of real 'pornography', was, of course, entirely covert, as was the production. Most material came in from the continent, or was pre-war, but Bernd assured me there was a reasonable business in at least local reproduction, if not origination. The secret was simply to utilise the legitimate daytime facilities – print works, process laboratories, studios – at night. In this, the night staff were willing and rewarded conspirators, and their employers quite often complicit at arms length.

In the milieu, Bernd soon became Bernie. He also acquired the nickname 'Bernie the Nazi'. This was to distinguish him from other Bernies in the area – most of whom were Jewish. His personal style rapidly became honed. He cultivated a relaxed, laconic manner, played to the slightly exotic nature of his parentage and balanced all with quiet effectiveness in his dealings. He acquired a number of female admirers, usually older than he, his time with Noreen having given him considerable sophistication in dealing with women. He did not like to become over-involved, however. Things were fine if they were fun. As he put it: 'I had the luck to come across three or four classy ladies – some theatrical, some in the restaurant business – who just wanted a regular fuck with a competent young man.' He also acquired a useful mentor in one of Hedda's regular clients: a senior police officer based in the West End. For whatever reason, this man took a liking to Bernd and, through contacts in the vice squad, was able to ensure a supply of films. It was a useful way of laundering pornography seized in raids and returning it to the original and suitably grateful owners. The contact also offered an early warning system for the occasional official visit the police felt obliged to make.

By the time of the Coronation and the Festival of Britain, Bernd was fully established as a player in the Soho scene. Life generally was improving. Markets and shops had begun to look more prosperous, the jazz clubs and theatres more full, the audiences better dressed. Film executives infiltrated the bohemians' pubs. London was getting its colour back. There was a frisson of concern on his eighteenth birthday, when his National Service call-up papers arrived. Eighteen months in the army was not in either Hedda's or Bernd's plans. Fortunately, Bernd's police mentor was able to ensure his exemption on the simple grounds that he was a resident alien, not a British citizen, and of monocular status. If not an essential intervention, it speeded up the process.

As Bernd himself acknowledged, his was a perfectly agreeable way of life. He had no great ambition, but had begun to take an interest in film. His work in the covert world of blue movies had included editing imported films. He developed a good grasp of technique and although both blasé about and critical of the quality of the material he handled, he began to think about how it might be done better. A particular passion was the classic 'B' movie. In those days, they were usually American crime stories shot in black and white, of course. Bernd loved the way they were lit and the implicit hard, soulless nature of the drama. For him, the women in the story, whether victims or molls, were highly sexual, tough creatures. Much like many of the women he met in Soho. But more 'arty' films, especially *roman policier* and *film noir*, were also appearing from the continent and, years later, Bernd was clear that *Fick Alles* had drawn heavily on his teenage fusion of the work of both minor American and French directors of the genre. He was an especial admirer of Jacques Rivette and later Chabrol, and it is sad that Töst's work was never very well received in France.

Whilst he had yet fully to formulate his ideas, or even commit himself to a career as a film maker, Bernd was developing his critical faculties as well as his thoughts on technique. Always reluctant to be too introspective, and suspicious of words like 'philosophy', Bernd also admits to this being the time when his general beliefs about life and its relationship to film became more coherent to him. If the films he brought to Hedda's were in his view 'garbage', this could not be said of Candy Barr's *Smart Aleck*. I reminded Bernd of this film during one of our long phone calls and he laughed. 'Yes, it was good. I won't say it was an influence but it stood out. Most stuff at the time was stuck in the twenties and thirties stag night culture. In fact a lot of it was made then. Yeah, possibly she got me seriously interested in making my own films.'

Somewhere around the mid-fifties, Bernd got his first chance to direct – or more accurately shoot, since they were the same role – his first porn film. The importers and distributors of the films Bernd regularly edited were, of course, local criminals, not film producers. One of these, a genial villain known as Jim the Grim (his family name was Reaper), called into the club and asked Bernd if he could 'knock out some fresh material'. As Bernd recalls it, Jim said, 'You're always belly-aching about how crap some of our stuff is, so why don't you have a go?' Bernd recruited what he described as 'two presentable tarts' and an Italian waiter with a reputation for sexual voracity. Italians were to feature frequently in his cast list. He was of the opinion this was because of their sexual vanity and insouciance. He borrowed some bits and pieces, dressed one of the upstairs rooms at Hedda's in a rough approximation of a French boudoir and shot two hours of film one evening. 'We had a lot of fun. Everyone got it on and I was able to cut six 20-minute loops from it. Jim was delighted, but frankly it looked like hell. 8mm is no way to make films and that decided me to go for 16mm. There'd been some pioneering work but 8mm shorts were still the norm. In fact the operating word was short.'

Bernd made several of these 'composites' as he called them. His skill was to have the performers develop their sexual encounters – singly, in pairs, as a trio or whatever – so that each phase could become its own film. Jim the Grim was more than pleased and Bernd made some useful money; enough in fact to buy a car – a second-hand Ford V8 Pilot. Jim would not, however, fund the development into 16mm. Bernd was very keen to get better quality. Lighting, magnetic sound and, of course, despite his lasting love for black and white – the obvious merits of colour.

Also slightly problematic, aged about nine or ten, Minou had by this time become an almost inseparable companion. She was not especially sheltered from her surroundings. Neither was she exposed to their full-frontal character. School over for the day, she demanded constantly to know why she could not accompany BB when he went off to make his films or to the editing studio. The explanation that she would be bored did not satisfy. She knew that the films had men and ladies taking their clothes off and she thought that sounded interesting. Bernd had avoided discussion of Minou in any detail until near the end of our relationship and, as it turned out, his life. He was vague about when Minou first accompanied him to an edit, but the girl can only have been ten or eleven at most. He said she had been interested for a few minutes and then demanded something to read. 'It was interesting but then it all got the same,' was her reported verdict. Bernd would not allow her into any of his live filming, but Minou became a regular in whichever lounge, side room or adjacent cafe was used as a rest area for cast and crew. As had Bernd, the little girl grew up as a habitué of a society of morally dangerous characters, all of whom treated her with great affection and care. Louis Bates recounts that, arriving home later than expected from a film shoot, Minou explained to her mother that, 'It took ages 'cos the man couldn't get it up. But this lady in her underwear made me cocoa.'

In 1957, Bernd at last persuaded Jim Reaper and his – now retired – policeman mentor to fund a 16mm production. It was still a budget production, but film stock, lights, optical work and editing were all relatively costly. There had been a debate over colour but the budget was tight and Bernd said it would work well in black and white. On a sunny June day, Bernd drove himself and his three actors out to the countryside around Dorking. Here there was a cottage with a barn, owned by a client and admirer of Hedda. With costumes hired from Berman's, they enacted the old tale of the maid, the groom and the lady. Bernd said that these threesomes were the surefire formula for audience appeal. The groom was played by Bernd's reliable Italian; the maid by another regular. The lady was an amateur. A senior nurse at the Women's Hospital on Soho Square, she was one of Bernd's personal intimates and quite evidently of a racy temperament. The film has long been lost, but Bernd said he remembered it vividly. 'I had this evolution thing, you know, maid alone feeling horny, groom watching and getting hard-on, then they get it together, then the lady comes across them, moment of confrontation and then the threesome. Well, the nurse is sort of nervous but keen. So she's watching and I see her licking her lips and she gets flushed and begins to pant a little and starts to feel herself up. She was a good-looking girl, early thirties, I guess. So then of course this is on the film now and without me saying anything, she's got her riding whip and she's fucking herself with it. Next, down on her knees sucking the groom off and, in between gobbles, begging the maid to thrash her. It's now out of control because they're all sexed up as hell and I'm leaping about trying to get it all. They manage to keep at it for an hour – God knows how. We've had it all, including sodomy, orgasms all round and a golden shower. The editing was a nightmare but, I have to say, it was pretty damn good.'

Jim the Grim was horrified. Apart from the fact that he thought black and white too arty-farty, he was not going to get his usual three or four loops for the price of one. What he had, was nearly 60 minutes of somewhat unusual movie. He was also deeply shocked by the anal sex and the golden shower. 'That's obscene, we could all go to jail for that,' he said. Persuaded at least to show the film to an invited group at Hedda's, he took great delight in pointing out to Bernd that the audience were less than enthusiastic. 'They don't like this sort of thing,' he said. A few weeks later he came into the editing suite where Bernd was finishing adjustments to another import. 'I've sold that film to a Dutch geezer,' he announced. 'So at least I got our money back and there's a pony in it for you, you lucky sod.'

The Dutch geezer was in fact Danish, and his name was Lasse Braun. For Bernd, the 16mm experiment had been his epiphany. He said, 'I knew it was the way to go, and that the old formulae were sterile.' Bernd never made any more multiple loops for Jim or anyone else in the UK. Grateful for the chance he'd had in Soho, he felt stifled by Britain's puritan hypocrisy and aversion to change. Unsurprisingly and, as it turned out, presciently, it was to Denmark that he returned; and where in 1958 he produced his first work as credited director.

The move was not without trauma. Hedda and Minou were hugely upset. 'Hell,' said Töst, 'I would have stayed if I could. They were my family and of course I felt bad. But at 24 there were things I had to do. Maman said I was like my father. I didn't know whether that was good or bad. Minou wanted to come with me. I would have taken her but she was only twelve years old. Smart, older in her head, but it wasn't on. She wouldn't speak to me for days.'

Louis remembers the time similarly. He claims he restored relations between Minou and her brother by suggesting that when Bernd had found somewhere to live she could join him for a holiday, with Hedda too. Bernd acknowledged this might have been the case.

It is easy to forget that foreign travel was a minority activity then. Apart from anything else, there were still strict currency restrictions. Bernd said he couldn't remember what arrangements were made. He said: 'I got a boat from some god-forsaken port on the east coast with some bank notes in a body belt.' Louis, as ever, provided the information that Bernd had indeed sailed from Harwich to the Hook, and then by train to Copenhagen. He took his own savings and the proceeds of the sale of his Ford. I reminded Bernd that the Suez war was around that time. His response was as expected: 'I didn't give a fuck, not my war.'

The pleasure of travel for the young is its carelessness. Bernd felt at home in Denmark – not just because he could still speak Danish well enough to win acceptance, but because he found the culture sympathetic. He recounted his arrival at

Copenhagen station in company with a French girl he met on the train. As they stood in discussion of what to do next – it being late evening – a car pulled up and three young men greeted them and asked what they were doing. 'Next thing, we're at this party somewhere in the boondocks and having a ball. After which one thing leads to another and the French girl gets to fuck one of the Danes and I wake up in bed next to my new flatmate who is called Leena and is Finnish and very charming and easy to live with.'

Bernd was very clear about his reason for being in Denmark. 'There was this great pressure to liberalise. I didn't want to just be in the sex film business, I wanted to make films about sex.' He made early contact with Lasse Braun on the strength of Jim the Grim's sale of Bernd's 16mm movie. Braun was encouraging about the film and helpful about the general scene, but Bernd did not press the acquaintance. 'I respected the man, but he had his thing, I had mine. We needed our own space.'

Braun had been helpful enough to steer Bernd toward the sort of places and people where he would have the best chance of winning support for his project. It seemed odd that Braun himself was not the best contact. Bernd shrugged the idea off as absurd. He did not want any more mentors, or anyone who might seek to control him, however well-intentioned. It is therefore fairly astonishing that within a month of his arrival in Copenhagen, about May 1958, he had begun work on the *Liebe* trilogy. Its funding appears to have been entirely on credit. Artists, equipment suppliers, location providers and processing laboratories were all prepared to take a chance on the young Töst. That he was persuasive is evident. He also had credentials, although his output was not apparently demonstrated in the form of a 'show reel'. It is quite possible that Braun, something of a radical crusader himself, might have provided background endorsement. Then, too, the porn movie network would quite likely have ratified Bernd's claims: as Töst said in another context, 'Small world, Bruno.' Whatever the explanation, the *Liebe* series had been made and sold by mid-year.

Töst was cavalier about the production and its intricacies; and he was elusive about the financing. Pressed on some details he wrote to me: 'You must understand this was such easy stuff for me. I found the actors – one of them, by the way, was the French girl I met on the train – and then I just had them do what they enjoyed doing. It was just a fuck, you know. Maybe they were special because they didn't care if they were looked at – or maybe they liked that. I can't recall names. I think she was called Julie or something. The guy came along with her – a boyfriend. He was fine, good physique, control, performance and so forth. He was German, called Dieter, I think. We really didn't care about names. The other thing was they had this odd harmony in physical terms. I mean, they were both pale and thin – almost androgynous at first sight. Except she had a dark, slightly angular Mediterranean look and he was blond with quite a feminine mouth. So in some lights you really had a double take on their sex. I remember she had black hair under her armpits and we had her trim some of her bush. I like a hairy groin, but even for black and white the camera needs some pink and hers was good. Anyway, all that was necessary was to let them do it in pleasant surroundings while I wandered about as discreetly as I could, to record the proceedings. It's the art of documentary.'

Julie and Dieter went on to star in all three films in the series. In the same letter, Töst said: 'These two loved to fuck. I don't know how sincere the relationship was, but they had real physical rapport – they were only 22 or so and had this incredible physical thing for each other. The screwing and oral was easy. Except the oral left him with teeth marks in his dick and a cut lip when she'd bucked up into his mouth. They had two days off for that. The anal made them think and was harder. I mean, there's the shit thing, and we weren't so formalised about enemas and colonic irrigation and so forth. Dieter had no problems. I wouldn't say he'd fuck anything but, well, he was a stud. Julie took a little time. She was a French woman *bien entendue* so I think hygiene came into it. I think in some way there was a power play between them – at times they seemed more to be fighting than fucking and the anal was also possibly too submissive for her. Or maybe she liked that aspect. But between us, Dieter and I kind of seduced her into it. Women can say absolutely no. But it's the 'maybe' that's always amazed me. Women don't just give in; they kind of take it all on board. That girl, woman, lady, person, whatever: she went into it saying so let's do it, and came – literally – out of it saying that was better than OK.'

The *Liebe* series, which became treasured by collectors, was not initially a great commercial success – though it made acceptable money. Each film focused exclusively on one aspect or perspective of the sexual act. They are all, in essence, about the act of looking into the act of sex. Töst was very explicit on this topic. He rejected the idea that somehow men were only voyeurs and that women 'felt' rather than 'looked'. 'Of course women look,' he said. 'They look in your eyes, they watch when your dick slides into their pussy, they hold your prick up to watch it when they give you a blow job, they turn round to look when you give it to them from behind. They look at each other the whole time. If they can't look, they touch. I sometimes think it is men who don't look and aren't too good at touch either.'

In *Fotze Liebe* we observe from the male perspective as first eyes, then mouth and penis engage with the woman's vulva. Bernd said he would have liked to remake this film with a lesbian sequence. Asked why, he responded, 'Gay sex is special because girls and guys have a unique knowledge of cunts and cocks, so they are in some degree making love to themselves.' In *Schwanz Liebe*, it is the woman's view as she engages in fellatio or is penetrated by the man. With *Arsch Liebe* both perspectives are engaged in exploring the experience of anal sex – though the woman is more closely observed in her reactions. Töst gave his films German titles partly because Germany was a big market at the time, and partly because, as he said, 'Ask Norman Mailer why German girls and the German language are so sexy. It's the Saxon thing. Don't forget, I have a lot of the Teuton in me too.'

At one level, these films seem artless enough. Shot in black and white 16mm the effect is reminiscent of cheap exploitation loops; but Bernd has lit and processed the product so that there is pin-sharp focus and the combination of stark contrast and subtlety he so liked in classic black and white movies. He uses the conventions of porn films to establish the *mise en scène*. That is, a woman in an apartment and some inference that she is feeling sexy and maybe awaiting a lover. Bernd's classic opening for a woman is for her to be lying on a sofa, her hand between her thighs with her skirt raised and underwear disarranged so that there is a glimpse of cunt as she masturbates. There may be an inference of heat, via a revolving fan or sweat on the skin; or the use of alcohol through the presence of ice, a glass and a bottle. His briefly suggested interiors are always disarranged. An open drawer, a disordered dressing table, wet soap in an empty bath. For men he often uses a shower sequence shot from behind with a brief body turn to flash – as it were – a semi-erect penis. The arrival of the other actor or actors rapidly leads to some minimal dialogue, the divestment of clothing and the sexual activity that is the purpose of the film. In this case, primarily, extreme close-up at great length of oral and genital interaction. This is intercut with periods of facial or other bodily responses during and at the completion of the sexual act.

Töst had established his credentials well enough to secure distribution. *Liebe* attracted some favourable interest in the fledgling industry; if only for its length and technical quality. At that time Denmark was on the cusp of liberalisation, as was much of the rest of continental Europe. Even so, pornography was still illicit and its distribution very much a covert and chancy affair. Despite this, Töst earned some money and received commissions to do more films, some on his beloved 16mm.

Back in London, Hedda continued to manage her club fairly successfully, despite changes in the social climate and with competition from other types of establishment.

The young film and advertising people who began populating Soho were not really interested in clubs like Hedda's, except as a curiosity. The founder members were dropping out as age crept up on them. The police too, although still corrupt enough, had formed new alliances within the zeitgeist. Bernd's old mentor had gone to live in Marbella – an early pioneer of that now outré resort. Minou, on the edge of puberty, was turning into a teenager. A very useful event was the demise of Hedda's Maltese landlord. He was shot in the head at his home in Hampstead Garden suburb, because of a gangland feud, it was supposed.

This left Hedda in full and clear possession of freehold in two houses in Meard Street. By happy chance, some months previously, the Maltese had transferred title to Hedda for fiscal reasons of his own. There was a document, held by Hedda, which also recorded her obligation to transfer title back if requested. No such request seems ever to have been made. With no rent to pay, Hedda was able to earn a reasonable living from the club's drink and food sales. One of her admirers gave her some sound business advice and, with the benefit of her club licence, she was able to move more into the mainstream as simply a private gentleman's club.

Bernd did not return to England during this period. He, Hedda and Minou kept up a frequent and lively correspondence. Minou especially wrote long, unaffected and rather charming letters to her BB. She shared her thoughts artlessly – these included ruminations on the character of her schoolteachers, most of whom she hated – and sometimes rebuked Bernd for deserting her. She always ended, though, with a row of kisses.

In the Spring of 1959 Hedda and Minou arrived in Copenhagen. Leena had returned to Finland. Her relationship with Bernd had been affectionate but in the end a matter of pleasant convenience for both of them. He was therefore left in possession of the apartment with its spare bedroom and could offer his mother and sister reasonable accommodation. After a few days enjoying Copenhagen, Bernd borrowed a car and the three of them set off for North Frisia. Bernd does not recall it as of great interest to him. He missed the city and found the bleakness of the islands oppressive. He does acknowledge being somewhat moved by his maman's genuine, if highly sentimental, exposition of her love affair with his father, Jurgen.

Back in Copenhagen, Hedda prepared to return to London. Minou prepared to stay with Bernd. There was no great dispute, Hedda being more concerned that Minou would continue some form of education than with separation from her daughter. Apparently, she consulted Louis, who advised her that, since Bernd was a competent young man, there should be nothing to worry about. Hedda therefore gave her consent. Louis was fairly certain that another of Hedda's male friends was rather more than that, and that Hedda was looking forward to the freedom due to a widow in the prime of life.

Minou was, of course, hugely pleased by all this. She decided that she could look after Bernd better than any mother or wife would. Refusing to register for school, she took on the persona of housekeeper and personal assistant with enthusiasm and success. 'She did one hell of a job,' said Bernd when we spoke about this period. 'I ate well, looked presentable and never missed an appointment – and the kid was only thirteen.'

Bernd was in regular work, shooting and directing two or three Super-8mm sex shorts each week in Denmark and Germany. It wasn't the work he wanted to do, but it was useful money until he could develop another project.

The *Liebe* series had been distinguished by stylistic quirks and flourishes – some major, others hardly noticeable – that lifted these works above the rest of his fellow pornographers' output: at the time and arguably forever. They certainly influenced American directors in the 1970s before video changed the genre completely.

Even so, it can also be argued that with *Liebe*, Töst anticipated many of the styles and trends that infused the evolution of video porn through to the nineties and beyond.

These included the combination of conventional minimalist narrative situations with strong, simplistic contextual cues and the use of amateurs, anticipating *Gonzo* and home-made videos. Where he remained apart was in his preference for what he described as 'real fur, real juice'. Moreover, his unique mark was the subtext that always gave edge to his movies as true cinéma-vérité.

To some extent, history repeats itself, but Töst brought technical innovation and genuine feeling for the drama and earthiness of the sexual act, too often lacking in the later mass-produced depilated world of commercial video hardcore. Such qualities were not much appreciated by the producers or their distributors – often the same people – but somehow Bernd usually managed to persuade them. As he once said to the lighting cameraman he liked to use where possible: 'They moan about the cost, but they always come to my previews and ask for a personal print.'

He also had a good eye for actors. 'They must like to fuck,' he said, 'and they must feel I want to make them look and feel good.' That said, he hated overacting. Not for Bernd the simulated groans and sighs. 'Fuck and suck and make the noises and say the stuff you want to say,' were his instructions. 'If you just want to pant, that's fine.'

He liked to know if the performers had already got a relationship or were new to each other, and would always allow time for them to get acquainted or become warmed up.

For what is usually called the 'money shot' he preferred never to allow the man to masturbate over the woman. If he was going to come over her face, into her mouth, on her breasts or wherever, she had to be the one to finish him. 'You get that intensity of look, like a sort of fond fascination when women are in charge of the orgasm,' he said. Or, if they were fucking, the man could come over her vulva unaided or even inside her. He liked the post-coital look of the vagina and made no concessions to what he called pornographers' cliché. 'The audience takes what I give,' Bernd would say. 'These are my actors and they should come how they like to come.' He added: 'If you compare good written porn with film, you see how limited film porn has become. A writer has to share his imagination – so should a film director.' He was also critical of the pressures to adopt standard, maximum visibility positions. 'Of course I like to get the camera in close with the right light. That's my problem. Most of all it has to be about the actors having a great fuck or whatever. A little wider on the thigh, hold that position and so forth, but not to interfere with the rapport. People know what they're watching, even the jerk-offs. Though real can frighten some people.'

I had been keen to have Bernd talk to me more about his life with Minou, in this period and later. He fended me off for nearly two years, saying, 'We got on well, she made a big difference to my life.' One day, Louis rang me up and said that Bernd liked the way I was handling his story and what I had written so far. He had come to the conclusion that he had to allow Minou her real place in the history and had written a long piece about it for me to include. He said it could be edited for style, but not to cut anything out. Early in 2001, the typescript arrived. It is reproduced here, pretty much as Bernd wrote it.

'From where we are now, this may seem a pretty bad story to tell. I can see all the fucking social workers reaching for their moral outrage. Fuck 'em. Minou was the best thing that happened to me.

'So, suddenly I have my little sister being very grown-up and keeping house and getting business for me. She was tall for her age and very cute in an elfin sort of way. Everyone knew she was my kid sister and that was OK too. She came with me quite a good deal on trips and to shoots. She knew how everything worked so that was no problem. In fact she was a fine judge of talent and of film. It all carried on smoothly for months. Maman was having a good time in London and we were in regular correspondence – though we kind of slid round the school thing. That said, Minou read widely and we kept up with languages and so forth. Then one day I was loafing around reading or whatever and there's a shriek from the bathroom. It's Minou. I jump up and ask what's the matter. "I'm leaking blood," she says. "Aha," I reply, "you're menstruating – congratulations." She pops her head round the door. "I know all that," she says. "Get me some towels or something." Next thing I'm in the chemist getting advice on what's suitable for a thirteen-year-old and then I'm back home.

So all is well and Minou is relaxed and saying, "I'm a woman now but my tits are so small". I reassure her about the tits and she says, "Well as long as you like them, that's all right." We laugh and go out to eat and she's chattering away and I think, "We're a couple." It feels good. Here is a person I don't have to pretend to, who I've known all her life, who loves me with no ifs and buts. So she's my sister, but that's what families are for. I want you to realise this was not a sex moment. She was my kid sister and buddy. I'd changed her nappy and now I was sharing her first period.

'In 1960, on the 8th of May to be precise, maman was killed in a car crash. Louis telephoned in the evening to tell me. He was pretty cut up and I found myself saying, "OK, Louis, it'll be OK." How stupid. She'd been with some guy, a good friend, and they were on the Hog's Back – a crap road somewhere in, is it Surrey? Anyway, I find out this road has a lousy reputation and they had been to lunch and he was driving, too fast probably, in his limo, and they just went off the road and into the trees and that was it. I tell Minou and we sit with our arms round each other crying. That night, I'm in bed, wide awake and Minou comes in and asks if she can stay in the bed with me. Of course she can. So we lie with our arms round each other and I'm stroking her hair and I kiss her cheek, which is wet with tears. She puts her arms round me and I hug her and I can feel her body and she's saying, "We mustn't ever be parted, BB." I tell her I love her, and then she kisses me and it's suddenly a woman's kiss, which goes on and I realise it is now a sex thing too, from all the love and the grief. I have a hard-on that I'm trying to keep away from her body, which is difficult but she doesn't seem to notice. Then she sighs and relaxes and just turns over and goes to sleep. Except for when we were in London for the funeral we always shared the same bed, but nothing happened as they say. We just carried on as before.'

The funeral was held, by odd chance, at St Magnus the Martyr in the City of London. Hedda had no church, but her lover, some form of banking figure, had family connections. Louis describes the occasion as one of the more bizarre events in his life. The lover's family, perhaps prompted by a sense of duty, as it was their scion who had killed the pair, offered the Tösts a shared event. In truth it was more of a memorial than a funeral, since both corpses were cremated privately elsewhere the day before the service. Hedda would have been gratified by the turnout she achieved. Many quite great and not quite so good personages turned up, representing a wide sample of the Soho fraternity. They made an extraordinary contrast to the sedate entourage of upper-middle-class respectability on the other side of the aisle. Nonetheless, the priest – this was a high church place – made a sound Anglo-Catholic job of the dual ceremony without mawkishness or infelicity of reference to the lives and relationships being remembered. Louis noticed how quiet and composed both Bernd and Minou were; she, holding her brother's hand throughout. There was a hugely bibulous wake back at the club, which saw Minou drunk – albeit mildly – for the first time. Bernd says he remembers little, except that he was pleased there were so many people, but anxious to get away from England. He and Minou spent a few days in London dealing with Hedda's affairs. Louis was the executor of her Will. Her property had been left equally to Bernd and Minou. It was decided that the club had to close and the premises either let or sold. Louis was told simply to do what he thought best financially. Bernd and Minou collected the urn with their mother's ashes, and retreated to Copenhagen.

Bernd's letter continued:

'We didn't forget maman, but we put her in the box marked "Happy Memories" and got on with our lives. One day we took her ashes up to North Frisia and scattered them in the dunes where, possibly, I was conceived. It was too late or too far to drive back to Copenhagen so we stopped in some wayside hotel. It wasn't a bad place and we had a good room with a big bathroom. We had quite a cheering dinner and a bit of wine. Well, to cut to the chase, I am in bed reading and Min is in the bathroom, and she comes out naked and just leaps into bed with me and sort of winds herself round me. I am going "Hey, kid," but she just kisses me and says, "I know you fancy me, you had a big stiffy when we were in bed on that horrid night." Then her hand is inside my pyjamas and her fingers are round my cock. "You are all I want, BB," she says. "You make me happy so I'm going to make you happy."

'I was nonplussed to say the least. I told her I loved her, found her very beautiful but that she was my sister and not even fifteen. We could go to jail, I reminded her. She went "Phooey." Then she said, "We're only half. If we fuck it could be the Pietrowski half screwing the Jurgen Töst half." I pointed out this would make us gay – queer in those days. Somehow this made us both start to laugh. After which we were kissing, and she had my pyjama pants off and was giving the first blow job of her life. Which was very agreeable, and I just lay back and stroked her pretty body and thought this was kind of weird, but it felt natural and right. I told her I would do anything with her she wanted except fuck her. This I felt for some obscure reason would have to wait a little. She didn't like it but agreed anyway. Just before we fell asleep I said to her: "Min, I don't just love you, I'm absolutely one hundred percent in love with you." She just snuggled up and said, "You'll have lots of chances to prove it." I thought that was damn grown-up.

'So, we carried on, and there was enough money and I began to think about my next project, which was *Melanie*. Minou and I just settled in to what was effectively a marriage – albeit one with edge. Just to clear it out of the way, we fucked for the first time a few weeks later. There seemed no point in not as we were doing everything else. It went well. In our time together we had a great sex life but I'm not going to enumerate it for the world. It's none of their damn business.

'The film was still a way off, but Minou was a good collaborator. Our relationship gave us security, a closed-off self-sufficient protection. We got nourishment and creative inspiration from it. At that time there was no her, no me; only us. I owe a lot to her for the tone and the way the character in *Melanie* evolves. I think there is quite an amount of Minou in her – it is named for her, of course – but some of me also. She thought my work, especially *Liebe* – which she admired but didn't like so well – was too bleak, harsh. She wanted a softer feel. Well, maybe she was right, maybe not. We put together a more than respectable movie and a lot of the credit goes to her. Not that she'd want it now. Stuff goes on, but those years were special, very special. If you find Min, give her my love and say I hope she is as happy as she deserves. Tell her I'm sorry I wouldn't stay in touch. It was panic at losing the second of the two women I had loved best. Maybe the only two I loved forever. I'll end this in case I lose my nerve. BT.'

This turned out to be the last letter I received from Bernd, although we referred to it briefly in a phone call just before his death. At the time he added his signature to Louis', on a letter of release for the publisher's proofs of the book.

The *Blue Magazine Liebe* interview – reproduced in full in Appendix 1 – came at a time when America, like Europe, was beginning to sense the liberation of rock and roll and the contraceptive pill. The sex industry was, as ever, quick to spot an opportunity. Töst himself had begun to regard the USA as his real destination. 'Money, energy, the ability to organise,' he said. His work had already achieved notice. The *Liebe* series was well regarded in the business as being of high technical quality. *Melanie* had been previewed early in 1963, and received excellent notices in the underground media. Although Töst had paid several visits to the USA between 1959 and the time of the interview it was only after this that he elected to stay on, having had a work permit, but now seeking a resident alien visa. He described himself as a 'film technician'. American filmmakers, on the east coast at least, were receptive to new ideas from Europe. Whilst distribution was increasingly to fall into the hands of organised crime, production still had a cottage industry feel to it. There were no real barriers to acceptance. The porn directors regarded themselves as a band of buccaneers and rebels. If it wasn't high-minded, it was at least harmlessly subversive. The connection with organised crime was ignored as simply a fact of life.

Meanwhile, Bernd and Minou were working steadily on the development of the *Melanie* project. Their income was adequate – pooling resources from their inheritance and by the mundane work of routine sex shorts. Minou never quite accepted this aspect of Bernd's way of life. She thought it vulgar, second-rate and beneath her brother's talents. She did take enough interest to steer him away from assignments and material she really thought beneath him or overly deviant, and Töst was happy to let her do it.

Of their relationship then, an acquaintance noted, 'It was obviously very close, very affectionate. Minou seemed extremely mature and the two of them had a real feeling of security. No one speculated about the private side of their lives, but there was a lot of casual touching and eye contact, which could have suggested a more sexual rapport. Who cared?'

Chapter 3
Apotheosis, New York & *Melanie*, 1962 – 1975

Whilst pornographic films were to remain illegal even in Denmark until the end of the 1960s; the industry was evolving quite rapidly. Töst was very much part of the new generation of makers. His time spent working reliably and competently on the staple products gave him a wide circle of well-disposed colleagues. Some were filmmakers, or at least producers themselves, others were distributors. It was in any case a small world where most people knew of each other.

Louis Bates saw little of Bernd in those days. He did, however, see Minou regularly on matters associated with the estate. He says she seemed very happy, self-assured and full of her role as her brother's confidante. Töst left her entirely free to manage their financial affairs and it was Minou who had advised the sale of the Meard Street property. Soho was coming up in the world and prices had risen considerably. With Louis' counsel, however, she elected to create a long leasehold but retain the freehold of the premises.

Töst meanwhile began to spend more time in America, culminating in his application for resident alien status. Minou had been comfortable with his shorter absences, but neither of them could contemplate a lengthy parting. It was this that probably also triggered her decision to divest them both of their British assets. We have also to remember that her relationship with her brother was at its most intense. Aged barely fifteen she joined Töst in Greenwich Village in 1961, travelling steerage on a French liner and entering the USA on a visitor's visa. Quite how she was able to prolong, if not regularise, her status in America is uncertain. However, she seems to have done so. Dwight Brimley[5], who at that time worked for Bernd's new mentor, Guido Stampetti, but not yet with Töst, opined that his employer's contacts would probably have been helpful.

Both the Tösts became rapidly acclimatised to Manhattan and the Village. From a base at the Chelsea, Minou soon hunted out a loft they could afford. Despite having a quite large sum available from the Soho sale, Minou was a prudent housekeeper. They were not poor, though. Minou was thrilled with Fifth Avenue and, encouraged by Bernd, happily spent a little time and cash in some of the elegant department stores on that street. Bernd himself was most often working, either on his own project, or to earn money. At weekends his pleasure was to have brunch with his beloved sister at the Russian Tea Room, or tea at the Plaza, or cocktails in the Algonquin.

Dwight had become acquainted with them both

---

[5]*Dwight Brimley*: Töst's driver, minder and subsequently long-term friend from the early 1960s when Töst first went to America. An ex-truck driver, Dwight was loaned to Töst when *Melanie* was being made. Dwight recalled, 'I did some moonlighting as a chauffeur bodyguard for a guy called Stampetti, who was a big wheel, in porn distribution among other things, in Brooklyn. He had hired Bernd and we kind of got along. So as I had a family and trucking was kind of demanding, I stayed with the guy. When he was in funds he was real generous and he treated me like a pal. I guess we had fun and it was a kind of interesting life so all in all I came out even. Don't print this, but I got to be in one of his movies. That was because I gave him a hard time about not using African-Americans. Mind you, there were some years, later, when he couldn't hardly pay the rent. Fortunately, I had a good business by then, so I could help out. He paid me back in the end though and I respect him a great deal for that.'

sometime during this first year, through chauffeuring them to Stampetti's offices or Brooklyn home. Stampetti, whose business interests included pornography, had taken to Bernd and, with his wife, adopted the couple whom they regarded rather as orphans. 'They thought it was just the right thing that Bernd took such care of his sister,' said Dwight. 'She was certainly cute. There was this odd mix of adult and kid in her – very charming. Mrs Stampetti was somewhat concerned about the girl getting involved in the movie business, but she trusted Bernd and her husband.'

By the beginning of 1962 the *Melanie* project had taken shape and the Manhattan-based sequences had been shot. It was Minou who had given her own name to the film and who discovered 'Melanie' – or rather, Lorraine Pewsey, whom she had spotted in a small burlesque theatre in Tribeca. By now, Dwight was driving Bernd and Minou regularly. Stampetti had decided to support the *Melanie* project and Dwight's role was to mind everyone's interests. It was he who took Minou to the theatre where she saw Lorraine. He said, 'The kid knew what she was doing. Lorraine was dead right for the part. Min told me Bernd would think the girl too busty but he'd be won over by the screen test. She was right on all counts. To be fair to Bernd, he was nice to Lorraine and very gracious to Minou. Not that she could do anything wrong in his eyes.'

Inevitably, Dwight became aware of the true situation in the Töst household. Perhaps surprisingly the two of them took no great trouble to hide it. Even in Copenhagen they had maintained a two-bedroom fiction. In their loft and in the supposed anonymity of Manhattan they installed a big double bed and lived as a normal couple. That Bernd could have had a lengthy jail term and Minou been locked up in a house of correction for wayward girls did not seem to have occurred to them. As a visitor to the apartment as well as a frequent companion, Dwight soon drew his own conclusions. 'I said to them, be careful. Don't let Stampetti find out – and don't make any enemies. They were nice kids.'

The project nearly ran into trouble in May. Stampetti liked the rough-cuts from the American sequences – a late snowfall in March had made the opening street scene memorable – but suddenly turned against the trip to France. The discussion with Bernd was lively. Why abroad anyway, Stampetti wanted to know, and why France? What was wrong with Italy? The rationale of international appeal and the French location being free and Bernd not speaking Italian did not sway Stampetti. He gave in only when Minou burst into tears and said she had set her heart on France. Since Stampetti had not actually put his hand in his pocket so far, and was simply guaranteeing costs, his leverage was limited. He agreed, with the proviso that there had to be at least one Italian in the film. 'A real stud,' he added. This gave the Tösts an added problem since they were reliant on their Copenhagen or Dutch contacts to provide candidates for the French sequences. Usually it didn't much matter what nationality, but inevitably they were likely to be northern European. In the event, the second female lead was French and they found the Italian on the way south. Quizzed about Lorraine, he reflected: 'Minou was right about my reservations. That said, Lorraine was a very sexy lady and a nice person. I had no problems with her. Also, you know, how people present in as you might say normal life versus what happens when they are fucking is quite different. This is especially true for women, I think. Women in sexual contexts transform; they have so much more in their physical reactions. With men it's the dick and some kind of grunts or exclamations. Women have nipples, vulva, skin, limbs and this range of facial and oral expressions that make it almost Shakespearean. Lorraine had tits that danced and the sexual face of a diva.'

Transatlantic travel was both more costly and more time consuming than it is today. Going by sea was still a favoured form of transport and the first jets were only just coming into service. Bernd and Minou decided to go with Lorraine by sea via Southampton. Stampetti had Dwight drive them to the docks and thoughtfully paid for two second-class cabins. Minou and Lorraine, of course, shared. They reached Copenhagen by air from London. In Copenhagen they reviewed the casting and selected the second female lead, Rosita, and two other couples used to working together.

Töst recalls being under considerable stress for the first time. The project was suddenly more complex and formidable in organisation than he had imagined. He wrote to me: 'Of course we had to do it all ourselves. Budgets were tight and there was no real professional infrastructure for this. We were responsible for all these people and equipment and film stock. Minou was outstanding. She tried to protect me as far as she could but it was hard. We also missed each other because we had to live apart in the physical sense, so there wasn't that intimacy. I think she minded less than me, but even so there were occasions when she'd creep into my room in the middle of the night just for a hug.'

They eventually set off for France in a decommissioned

ambulance driven by Bernd. It was very cramped, with six people and the film equipment in the back. It was also very slow. When Rosita Dumarnier – as she had become – and I met in New York for the actors' reunion, she told me: 'It was horribly uncomfortable, but Bernd and Minou always made sure we had a good place to stay for the night and a good dinner. I have to say, we often became quite drunk and the hotels must have wondered who these crazy people were. Of course, we said we were film people and that explained all. We never said what sort of film though. Minou made sure that Lorraine and I got to know each other so by the time we reached Provence we were good friends and already had our roles in mind. In fact we had slept together. It was not my first experience of a woman, but certainly a very pleasurable one. It was a happy group, I remember.'

Töst himself had more dour memories, at least of the journey. 'Fucking uncomfortable, expensive and long,' was his verdict. The destination was a small chateau or rather, large manoir, some thirty miles south-east of Avignon. Owned by a friend of Jim the Grim, it had been loaned for free, on condition that a print of the movie would be made available in the UK on a similar basis. Töst calculated that the lost revenues would be minimal, given the current state of the British pornographic film business.

Four days after leaving Copenhagen they arrived at the Manoir des Sangliers. The Italian had finally been acquired in a bar in Avignon. It was June, the weather truly Proven¢al. As Töst said, 'In a place like that, all you want is a glass of wine, no clothes and a great fuck.' Minou excelled herself as their housekeeper and cook. Töst was genial, and the cast did what they were there to do with considerable spirit, including the

S&M fantasies. Despite Töst's reservations about the film, it is undoubtedly his cheeriest work, and one that did make him good money. In retrospect, something else seemed to infuse his attitude when it came up in conversation. The truth now understood is that this sojourn in France was the beginning of the end for Bernd and Minou.

A correspondence, albeit sporadic, had always been maintained between Louis and Minou. The former showed me a letter from her he received in September 1962. In it she refers to some minor business matters but continues: 'The film went so very well and Bernd was at his best – even though I think he is still not sure about the style. The cast were happy and well-fed. For the food I will take credit. Now we are back in New York and the film will be a success, I know. Dear Louis, I am so muddled and unhappy. In France I met a man with whom I think I must be in love. BB is the man I love more than the world. Can I also be in love with someone else?'

The man she met was a neighbour of the Manoir. He was French-Swiss and a professional vigneron with respectable hectares producing decent regional wines. Minou and he came across each other in the market in Apt. When finally, just before this book was due to go to press, I had traced Minou – or rather Louis, had decided to put me in touch – she talked about that meeting. 'I had been buying vegetables, olives; normal things. Henri was beside me at a stall. We reached for the same aubergine or something. Doesn't it always happen that way? I don't think he had an idea of how young I was, only just sixteen, you know. He didn't condescend, or flirt openly.

He was just charming. He was elegant and very grown-up, in a way that Bernd wasn't. I had this terrible feeling of disloyalty. There was my beloved brother who had done everything for me. He had been father, wonderful lover, companion and given my name to his film. Here I was looking at this stranger and thinking, knowing absolutely, I was in love.'

Louis recalls the letter, and his reply. In summary he told her to take the time to become sure of her feelings, but that it was entirely natural to look for a new relationship. One free of the past, able to provide her with children if that was what she wanted. He said he had no idea how Bernd would react, but supposed that if her brother loved her well enough he would be glad for her. Louis said, 'I felt very deeply for her, yet relieved. Even more, I was very uncomfortable at being an agony aunt. In fact, it was worse than that. I had begun to be bored with the Töst children and their legacy. Their milieu had nothing to do with me really. I had just fallen into it by accident, and, I suppose, fallen for Hedda's class of winsome exploitation. Bernd was, in truth, a rather spoilt little brat who never grew up. He certainly never showed me much gratitude. Minou I had some affection for, though frankly she was a facsimile of her mother. It would be, indeed was, quite appropriate for her to marry an older Swiss vigneron. Just deserts all round if you ask me.'

Melanie was released in late 1963 with considerable success in its marketplace. Stampetti was happy with the commercial result, if remaining unhappy with France. Töst also was content that his work had been well-received and even more so that his bank accounts were healthy. Matters between the brother and sister were also perfectly harmonious, it seems. Minou has confessed to a clandestine correspondence with Henri, conducted via a poste restante address in Manhattan. She is adamant that she never stopped loving Bernd, and it was this that enabled her to dissimulate in their relationship.

Bernd enjoyed a period of both leisure and modest celebrity. He did interviews, went to parties – often without Minou – and spent a considerable amount of time in bars. Neither Dwight, nor later Minou, were very willing to make adverse comment, but it seems probable that, at this time, Bernd was somewhat on the slide in his self-indulgences. The erosion of their closeness through his generally thoughtless behaviour must have, in its way, helped Minou to resolve her emotional conflict. She admitted that, whilst her love for her brother never wavered, she sometimes felt as if she had become Hedda for him. Early in 1964, immediately after her eighteenth birthday, Minou packed a suitcase, walked out of the loft and took a cab to the airport and an Air France 707 to Paris. She never saw or spoke to Bernd again. Her letters went unanswered and her invitations to visit were ignored.

That Töst was the loser and Minou the winner is unarguable, at least from a conventional viewpoint. She became the chatelaine of an estate and mother of three fine children. He made in quite quick succession four more films of some merit in their canon, which arguably, garnered less financial reward than they deserved. Then, apart from brief sightings, he effectively disappeared from view for the next 30 years or so and died, not so much embittered, as tired and saddened.

After Minou's departure – defection was the word Töst used – he began serious drinking. Dwight recounts how on numerous occasions he would be called to a bar where Töst had been for many hours and had at last fallen off his stool. Eventually, Dwight's patience with phone calls that always seemed to arrive just as he was going to bed, ran out. He said: 'I told him I was pissed at him for being a pain in the ass and in future he could crawl home or sleep it off in the drunk tank at the nearest precinct. You know, he looked at me, smiled, and said, "OK, Dwight, I guess you're right'.' The next day there were some flowers sent for my wife and a note saying sorry. He'd gone from the loft and we discovered later he had flown to Germany.'

Töst arrived in Berlin on a Pan Am flight via Frankfurt toward the end of 1964. What had prompted this journey is hard to discern. Quite possibly it was an escape from the loft and Greenwich Village, full as they were of Minou's presence. He must also have begun to evolve an idea for the film that became *Fick Alles*. It promised to be a hard winter and Berlin – even in the increasingly prosperous western sectors – was a harsh place to be. Töst still had a reasonable amount of money from his inheritance and *Melanie* so checked himself into the Hilton. Here, in the bar, he discovered the woman we know as Helga Divine. Since she was to have the central role in his life for the succeeding months she should tell her own story, much as she told it to me many years later when we met in New York. (See Appendix 2).

'To be honest, I was a hooker. Quite a classy one, I think, and the Hilton was a good place to meet men with money. West Berlin was a busy city with lots of officers, diplomats and business people; the *Untermenschen* were less visible. Bernd and I must have been about the same age so we both had not so good memories of the war. Mine were harder than his, I think. Some people believe that being a prostitute is a bad thing. It can be, but there are worse things than being screwed, and $100 for an hour or two in bed with some fat man was good money in those days. Some girls would still sell sex for cigarettes. I had an apartment in a nice house and a car. It is not *Pretty Woman*, this way of life, and the street is no place to find work. Anyway, Bernd came into the bar. He looked American – slightly untidy, not handsome – but he had a certain style. He was at the bar and we looked at each other and smiled. I think there was something we saw in each other. When he spoke, he had this fluent German – colloquial, I couldn't place it, not flawless, just very attractive. I asked him where he was from and he said New York. I ask, "How are things in New York?" And he replies, "Well, it surely isn't Plato's Republic." This makes me laugh. We have a couple of drinks and he says he is a film director. Oh, that story, I think. He says no, really, I make films about sex. I tell him that is most interesting but not to me. He just smiles and asks me why not, since I am obviously in the sex business. This is a shock for me. I dressed quite conservatively and I did not do anything to attract the client until they showed an interest. He says, "We are in the same business, we recognise each other." Well, after that I had to submit and we relax and he tells me about some of his films. I have seen *Liebe* and heard of *Melanie*. Not to be boring with this story we became friendly and ate dinner. After dinner I am looking at my watch and Töst says, "I know, you have wasted valuable revenue time – but maybe I have a proposal." I think, he wants a fuck, but he said,

"I would like you to be in the film that I plan to make in Berlin." I am a little doubtful until he offers me $10,000 for about five days of work. In fact, of course, it takes much more of my time, because Bernd asks for my help in casting and such matters as locations, which made my car useful. He knew film people in the city but seemed to trust me. Also, he said, you are the heroine so you must have choices. After a week or so he is tired of the Hilton and there is an apartment vacant for a while in my house on the floor below. He moves in. We are now quite good friends and have some laughs. I have still been seeing clients and Bernd was helpful by not asking things of me in the evenings. Then it is Christmas Eve and I say to Bernd we are both orphans and you are a stranger here, so shall we make our Christmas Eve together?

'It was a lot of fun and he told me about his life and about Minou and we took too much drink in a nice way. After that I invited him to my bed and we had a pleasant fuck. It was the only time we fucked. He never mentioned it or proposed it to me again, but I noticed he was always thoughtful during the filming. He would ask if all was OK and did I want to rest and those sort of things. I felt he was quite sad. These are not matters to discuss with our colleagues in the group.

'His methods were quite strange to me. His first meeting was with all of the cast. He gave us each a sheet of paper, which he said was the call sheet. It had each day the scene, and the location and who would be there. Each day he would arrive at the location with bits of paper, very badly written, and tell us the plan for the day. Then we would deal with our clothes and any make-up. He had a lighting cameraman, but no other crew, and they would set everything up themselves. Yes, and there was a nice girl to help the men if they needed it. She was also my partner in the lesbian scene. Although I had been involved with most of the casting, he did make some different choices. I was not so happy with one or two of them in the rape sequence but perhaps this made it more real. You know, I think Bernd was quite ruthless in his way.

'Before we began the filming Bernd would say some words about how he thought we should feel. These were always to the point and he made me realise how much anger I had in me and how much contempt for men. Equally, he made me understand how vengeful and full of dislike men often are for women. This made the scenes very powerful and quite disturbing. I wondered how they could possibly be erotic. Then when I saw myself on the screen, especially after the rape, I understood better. It was about the sexuality of power. Bernd never gave us a big philosophy. He'd just say things like, "This fat man just wants to jerk off over you while he watches you masturbate. Easy money." Or he'd say to the man, "You just want to fuck this sexy little whore until her ears fly off, and she is going to make you come so hard you'll tell her where you get the drugs from, and just maybe you know she wants to kill you."

'It was extraordinary when we did the rape scene on the bombsite. Bernd had a permit to film and the authorities sent two policemen, to keep an eye on us, I suppose. The authorities had no idea what the film really was; they were just told it was a documentary drama. Of course we could not have them watch, so Bernd explained I would have to remove my top and out of respect the set must be cleared of everyone except himself and the actors. Well, this made me laugh, until Bernd took my arm and said, "You're about to be gang-banged, Fräulein; let's see how funny you find that." I can tell you, it was frightening.

I had prepared for a scene where just two men would have sex with me because I wanted something from them – drugs, information, who knows. Suddenly three more appear. I shall always remember the smell of that horrible old sofa they made me lie on. I can tell you, I had wondered whether I could make it seem real when I had to shoot the two men. By the time they finished I wished the gun had real bullets. I loved watching them fall down and this fake blood from under their shirts that should have been real.

'Afterwards, Bernd was very thoughtful and considerate. It was dreadfully cold, but I shivered with other emotions. He put a coat around me, told me how wonderful I had been and sent me home in a taxi. He wouldn't let the other actors thank me – this was very perceptive of him. That had felt real and I hated them. I even hated Bernd for a moment. He invited me to a private screening of the first cut. It was just us two. He said nothing, we watched. I told him he had done a good job, but this was not a sex film. Of course not, he reminded me, it is a film about sex.

'It took him about two weeks to finish and after that I suppose he made arrangements for distribution. We met many times for coffee or a meal until he left Berlin, but I never heard from him after that until we met by chance at a film festival years later.'

Bernd made arrangements for continental distribution through his German contacts. *Fick Alles* was a cult hit and made Helga a minor celebrity; something that proved useful when she set up her own business. Bernd retained two prints and the out-takes. One print would go to London, where Jim Reaper maintained a friendly interest in Bernd; the other would return to the USA where Guido Stampetti would shake his head and mutter: 'Bernie, you forgot the main point.' The movie would get distribution, but was only well-received among certain intelligentsia and in fetish circles. In the UK, it went nowhere. An attempt was made in the early 1980s to show it in cinema clubs, but was frustrated by the police and moralist campaign groups.

Having spent the winter in Berlin, New York in February did not appeal. Dwight says that Töst appeared much more relaxed and together than he had been, and his drinking was under control. There was still money about and *Fick Alles* was contributing to the bank balance. Töst decided to find some sunshine and booked himself on a flight to Los Angeles. Apparently, he had no purpose in mind other than to get warm. His choice of LA may well have been its connection with the film business and it is possible that Stampetti had contacts there. The pornographic film trade was, however, much more underground than in New York. Even the well-known Alec de Renzy had not yet begun to make his 'beaver' shorts. In retrospect it is astonishing how ahead of his time Töst was, having made five seminal films by his early thirties.

Töst seemed to be back on track and fully operational after the break with Minou. Yet it was to be another four years before he released *Super Bitch in the Halls of the Sex Warriors*. This can partly be explained by his need to acclimatise to a new environment for filmmaking. People had to be met, contacts secured.

The legal and moral climate was also less helpful than in New York. Hollywood had its decadent side, but this was carefully concealed. Judges were not so easily suborned, Watch Committees more assiduous and the police decidedly invasive.

In fact, LA was, at heart, provincial. The portrait painted by Raymond Chandler was still valid. This part of California was a genuine whited sepulchre, and whatever games took place were definitely behind the oak doors of the elegant hillside houses and less agreeably behind the screen doors of the shotgun homes on the wrong side of the tracks.

In his line of work, the essential skill was making contact. Töst had this, so that very shortly he had rented an apartment in a reasonable part of town and was known in the sort of bars where aspiring actors and wannabe directors meet the intermediaries of the influential. Töst recalls this time with some pleasure.

'I enjoyed it; met some interesting people. Candy Barr, yes. Great lady, funny; getting older but still sexy. Alec de Renzy also I met. He was pretty amazed by the sort of movies I had been doing. He couldn't understand why I wasn't in jail. There were a couple of us – not de Renzy – just me, some actor waiting for a break and this producer. I won't say his name because he is now very famous and respected. He had been a success in the forties as well. He had seen *Liebe* in Europe, and *Melanie* at someone's house in LA. I'll call him Syd. He was something of a porn film nut; would love to have made them but of course had his reputation. Anyhow, the three of us got on and went about like college kids to bars where we picked up girls. I tell you, you could fuck six a day if you wanted. This is California, Hollywood, the whole hippie, pill, freedom schtick. We of course were film guys, talent scouts, file cabinets full of projects that required pretty girls. Syd had a real nice red Caddy convertible. Well, although he was loaded, we all wanted to pay our way, so the neat thing was to give the girls screen tests. Syd's home in the hills had a little studio, and it was all very impressive. To be honest, quite a lot of the tests were genuine in that we didn't just go, "Ha, now you're here, take your clothes off." We set it up properly, and the actor – Ray, I'll call him – would give them some lines and I would roll the camera. Then we'd be nice and offer them a cocktail and sit around for a bit and say we'd let them know. I can't recall the percentage, but the very frequent result was the girl fluttering her eyelashes and going, "Oh, kind sirs, is there nothing else I can do to impress you?" Actually, we always told the girl she could bring a chaperone, so then we had two of them cooing at us. Except once, when this kid brought her aunt. We did a piece of Shakespeare. If we got lucky, we'd shmooze the girl up for a strip and some nude work. If we got really lucky, the actor got to fuck the girl while we filmed that. That was cool except I had to avoid showing his face for obvious reasons and the girls weren't always adventurous so it could be samey. Still, there was a market for this stuff and it kept us in beer money. Most often though, we'd end up with the test, and a date with whomever of us the girl liked best. It was a good way to have a sex life. I have never ceased to be amazed at the way girls are. Why I am amazed escapes me. Life should have taught me different. I think it is because they are very contrary people, like cats. Treated right, one on one, they'll do absolutely anything, and usually enjoy it; if they like you, cock sucking is a no-brainer. A fuck is either a whim thing or kind of purposeful. Syd, who was divorced but had teenage kids, said to me once: "Hell, Bernie, I envy my son with all these women ahead of him. Trouble is, I also wonder if my daughter is like these girls – a secret tramp." I told him not to worry, better his kid liked sex than not. Plus, I said, all girls have a little of the tramp in them, it's how they get men. Just make sure your tramp of a kid mixes with the right people.'

According to Töst, this pleasant way of life continued for a couple of years. Then, in the summer of 1967, he decided he was bored and needed a new project. It was his friend Syd who gave him the idea. The censorship issue was evolving under pressure from a mix of social developments and commercial opportunism. In Europe, *I Am Curious Yellow* had made a real impact. The censorship laws in Denmark were about to be abandoned and, in Holland, Amsterdam was an almost open city. Even in the USA, the loophole of documentary meant that there was a difference between a pornographic film and a film about pornography. Syd suggested to Töst that, with so much sex not just for sale, but being given away by the young women of Los Angeles, there was an interesting movie to be made.

Töst told me: 'I thought that was quite good, but it didn't seem to go anywhere for me. All we had to do was string together stuff like we'd been doing for fun, add some interviews and a commentary and what would we have? It felt like a means of giving bank clerks something to go "tut-tut" about and jerk off at the same time. Then I thought, it's about the girls, they're the heroes. Then I read about these licensed brothels in Nevada and remembered my childhood. I thought, what a clown, the movie has been there all the time. The title idea came at the same time – I thought of these girls as sex warriors. "Super Bitch" came later. Syd liked the idea a lot and was good enough to offer to bankroll at least part of the film. He wanted to use 35mm, which is a real on-cost at all levels. Still, he told me he could get other backers if I used it, so I agreed if we could shoot 16mm and upgrade in the lab. In the end, after I had given Stampetti a cut – which he'd earned – and other slices necessary, I was left with ten per cent of the gross as my share, but that was OK. It worked, and it made sensible money.'

To set up the film was even more ambitious than *Melanie* had been. The idea, if it was to be executed credibly and above all as a quality product, required something special in the way of location and casting – as well as a larger production crew than Töst normally used. Syd and Ray between them were of great value in equipment, crew and at least an embryo cast list. What Töst wanted was the location, and he wanted it to be real. Apart from anything else, to rent a studio and build a set in LA would not only cost thousands of dollars, it would be highly risky.

Guido Stampetti provided the solution. His Las Vegas business associates had already begun to set up an out-of-town brothel in anticipation of a favourable state ruling.

In fact, the place was complete, partly staffed and idle only because of legal niceties. Stampetti arranged for Töst to visit and come to whatever agreement seemed appropriate. 'It cost me half my take on the gross,' said Töst, 'but it was worth it. The place was perfect in location and layout and decor. The madam who ran it was one tough bitch. So she was, of course, where the final title came from. It helped that I had grown up in and around a similar business. I told her about maman and this woman had tears in her eyes. I swear she wanted to adopt me. Anyway, we meet the girls she has there already and they are great and perfectly willing to be involved – as you would expect, I guess. This means we just ship in two or three of the best of our cast where we think either their looks or their specific sexual capabilities are needed. You know what I mean. There's always a bit of S&M, water, anal and so forth. Not everyone will do stuff. There again, these girls we interviewed in LA weren't hookers – for the most part. The young lady – I use the term advisedly – who was most willing to do anal was a convent girl from a weird-sounding place called de Funiak Springs in the Florida panhandle.'

Töst had less than four weeks before the lawyers were likely to open the doors of the brothel to paying guests. Only one problem remained; where to find the johns. The option of actors was not one that appealed. It cost more money and it lacked the verisimilitude Töst wanted – and needed – to make the documentary claim stick. Then it came to him: invite prospective customers to participate for free. The idea appealed to the madam and even more to the owners of the business. Töst left it to them to work out the details. 'All I wanted,' he said, 'was guys who were happy to get it on and wouldn't mind me.' He stopped and reflected for a moment when he said this. There was silence on the telephone line. Then he laughed and said, 'Hey, do you think I invented reality TV? I was amazed when they arrived at how cool they were about the whole thing. But I shouldn't have been.'

Töst took a great deal of time and trouble working with 'his' girls to configure the logistics of filming. He had a clear vision of the physical look he wanted to create, as well as the atmosphere. One week from 'L' day, as they named it – Bernd forgot why – and they were ready for the arrival of the guests and for the seven days of filming Töst had allocated. It was a success. According to Töst, no one backed out, broke down, complained or showed off. 'The girls were just total professionals,' he said.

'Even the convent girl had a great time – though she said she'd had enough dick in her ass to last a lifetime. It was the johns who amazed me. They came dressed like we asked, and they did their thing like the gentlemanly schmos they were, and they said thank you to the ladies and even left money in the staff gift box. I heard later that this place did gangbusters in business on the word of mouth. Best of all, two of the girls we brought up from LA stayed on as permanent staff. Not the convent girl though, neat as that would have been.'

The film went back to LA and into the labs and the editing suite. Syd kept interested and facilitated access to the technical facilities, though at arms' length. As anticipated, there were always enough underlings around big organisations happy to subvert the system for some extra money. In fact, Töst's major concern was not to lose copies to pirates. He therefore called Stampetti, who, on the grounds of protecting his investment, had Dwight flown out to help Töst guard the film at all stages of the process. Dwight enjoyed himself. 'It was easy work, if dull at times, but I got to see LA and something of the movie business and stayed in nice places. The Syd guy was OK. He showed us a good time. At the preview in his home we had the money people and the dame from the brothel and some other types I imagine were in distribution. Strictly, I should have been with the other chauffeurs and minders, but Töst said I was his head of security and went everywhere. One helluva movie: I was pretty amazed. I mean, you hear stuff about what guys like to do and, swell for them, but some of these cats, what to say! Was it sexy? Well, in parts of it for sure, and the girls were fine looking. It's kind of weird in a room full of businessmen though, and they're looking at it with dollar signs in their eyes. At the end there was some applause and backslapping and they shake Bernie by the hand and troop off in their limos.'

The film was a success. It made less money than *Melanie*, largely because European distribution was weaker and it had less appeal as a quasi-documentary. It did win great plaudits, however, for the art direction. In the USA, it slipped quietly into the underground market through 1969 and into 1970. Then, with significant changes occurring in the censorship climate, it emerged during 1971 as a real money-earner in several cities, especially New York. As with films such as *Deep Throat* and *Green Door* that came later, *Super Bitch* acquired something of an upscale and also college following. Perhaps because of title confusion with Russ Meyer's *Super Vixens*, Töst never quite got the credit he deserved. Nonetheless, his backers felt sufficiently confident of him, and the increasingly liberalised climate, to support his next project, which would become *The Absence of Real Desire*.

During one of our conversations, I asked Bernd if *Super Bitch*, or any of his previous films, had been entered for the famous Wet Dreams festivals held in Amsterdam in the early 1970s. He dismissed the idea with some acerbity. 'Those things showed mostly amateur crap set up by a bunch of drug-crazed, sexually immature hippies,' he snapped. 'Anyway, my distributors weren't interested and nor was I. I went to one from curiosity – forgotten which year, '70 or '71. You know, people had caught on to 16mm at last, though there were still large numbers of 8mm films and they were all so short. They had a terrible old fifties thing by Genet, which was pretentious crap, albeit 16mm, and some animal stuff, which was just freaky. There was that funny, spoof Disney *Snow White* cartoon, and that was it. I met a nice lady called Betty Dodson who was intelligent and thoughtful, and a good artist. Al Goldstein, whom I respected and liked, seemed to be the only guy with professional judgement there. Oddly, I knew, and had done a couple of loops for two guys called Oscar and Ziegfeld or somesuch. They won a prize for a decent enough cocksucking movie and we had a few drinks back in LA to celebrate. I don't think there were any very serious movie makers there. Most of it was, frankly, dreadful.' He added, 'One interesting technical thing was that I saw video porn for the first time. To be honest, I didn't see the potential.'

Dwight had long since returned to Brooklyn. Töst was very at home in LA and with the California scene. He stayed in touch with Syd – now with a major studio – and Ray, who had found work on a popular soap. It was whilst with them both in a bar in downtown LA that he met Cayman Montrose. She too had a private story to tell in our meeting at the Plaza.

'I was a friend of Ray's. We'd in fact done a couple of cheap porno films together. Nothing heavy, just suck and fuck in a motel room. He was a nice boy and we liked to fuck anyway. He had fallen on his feet and was now in good work. I was just mooching around and living off my allowance from Dad. It had occurred to me that this was a dangerous time for me. I mean, doing porn can take you down more than up. Ray said I should meet Syd and Bernie. Syd sounded cool as a producer in a big company. Bernie sounded less sensible, but Ray talked him up so we all met. I don't know what he had told Bernie but, after some general stuff, Syd and Ray take off and leave me with this European who sounds American and who makes seriously sexual films. I tried to leave but Bernie just looked at me and said, "I need to talk to someone intelligent and knowledgeable about aspects of California life. Ray said you would be excellent." Well, he has a winning manner when he tries so I listen while he tells me about his ideas about Valley girls and being rich, well-educated and bored, and the way sex is in that situation. I realise he has it spot on and it is me he is talking about. Me, and many of my friends: here in this wonderfully rich country full of opportunity, not knowing whether to start a revolution or get stoned and get laid. I told him he had it about right. Then he told me how he wanted to make a film on this topic and could I help him think it through and maybe choose the right cast. He said he had backers interested and told me something of his other films. I do remember his "about sex" line.

'I said I would not contemplate taking part and he just said, "Of course not, it's your advice I want." So because by now I'd had three martinis I got snippy and asked him why of course not and wasn't I sexy enough? He just grinned at me in that lopsided way – oddly, having the one eye made him very rakish and attractive, kind of battered – and said with a little German accent, "Liebchen, you are very sexy indeed, but you must do what you want to do."'

With Cayman – her real name, having been conceived in that island – as his adviser and subsequent star, Töst rapidly put together finance, cast and storyboards. He told me, 'I think my backers were more excited by this than by any other film I had proposed. It sounded just what they thought commercial – naked Californian guys and gals getting it on in the sunshine. Which, of course, is pretty much the way US porn went. Cayman put together a neat cast. I believe they were acquaintances if not friends. The girls all had blonde hair, blue eyes, shiny smiles, bouncy tits, firm asses and all that. The guys had the hair, the jawline, the pecs and naturally the dicks. I didn't want Latino and hairiness; I wanted WASP and preppy. I can't recall when Cayman decided she wanted a part. I think it was either when she realised how great the studs were, or when she understood the storyline.'

Cayman herself confesses it was a bit of both. 'I did find the people sexy; in fact, I'd already screwed one of the boys, and the story was interesting. Or at least it had a point to make. I guess, though, the intellectual thing was just there to sanction my having fun, and earning some real money.' The backers insisted on a 35mm upgrade again, despite Töst's efforts to persuade them that 16mm would be as good. Töst had his revenge by using 8mm for the black and white opening and closing split screen sequences.

Whilst the actors were impressed by the movie when Töst showed them his cut, the backers were less so. Töst says of the preview meeting: 'There was a certain amount of blood on the walls. They loved the shiny 35mm college sex and hated the 8mm black and white inserts, which I lit to be seedy and grainy. They were going – oh, Bernie, why spoil a great movie with that sleaze stuff. I said this is the movie I make. If you just want a six-pack stag movie, find yourself a tame hack to make it. They told me it was their movie and they'd take it away from me. I said, you think this is the only print? The master is in a safe deposit.' In the end, Bernd did a deal. The backers got a copy they could edit how they wanted and Bernd kept his original master and the freedom to distribute his version with a different title in New York, Chicago and Boston. Since the black and white inserts were something of a technical problem, the edited version finally emerged with some odd discontinuities in the opening and closing sequences. It was released in its 'commercial' version as *Sunshine Girls*.

The spat was not helpful: money was made by the distributors, but not by Töst, who had to be content with the basic per diems he was paid to direct. He left for New York, his home territory, with the film he had always privately called *The Absence of Real Desire*, to discuss a distribution deal with Guido Stampetti. He was out of luck.

Stampetti was dead; felled by a bowl of rigatoni on which he first choked and then, from the consequent convulsions, suffered a fatal heart attack. After a suitable mourning period, Töst felt able to approach the family consigliere, a Jewish attorney called Nussbaum. Personally unsympathetic to pornography, Nussbaum recognised that his deceased client had some financial interests to protect. He therefore transferred the Stampetti interests in the film to Töst, with a proviso that sixty per cent of the gross from whatever market source would accrue to his client's estate. Töst had little choice, or indeed interest, in a prolonged negotiation. He signed the papers and went to stay with Dwight, who had moved to Staten Island.

The problem now was to get distribution. Since he had left New York, the scene had changed. Not only had distribution muscle coalesced into a more organised form, the films themselves were changed. Censorship rules and enforcement were more liberal and the city-states of Eastern America now provided cinemas where 'adult movies' could be shown. The old porno loop remained the staple. Beyond that, the higher budget movie with, as it were, content, had begun to bring pornography into the sphere of the chattering classes.

Töst was fortunate in that Dwight knew Stampetti's contacts and, whilst he grumbled that Töst 'never had a black man or a black woman' in his films, proved a great friend and ally. I asked Dwight how Töst had reacted to the criticism of racism. The reply was, 'He was truly contrite, even sorrowful. He said it had just never occurred to him, and he had not often met black people in the business. I knew he wasn't a prejudiced guy. Then he said to me, I think black and white fucking is the exciting thing of the future, but it will have to carry a lot of baggage before we stop fantasising anything other than how big black dicks are. Which is when he gave me a part in a movie.'

In the end, with Dwight's help and by calling in some favours, they were able to sell the film to the group who had acquired some of Stampetti's legitimate commercial interests. The return for Töst was, if not nugatory, little better than subsistence. His losing run was enhanced by news from England that Jim Reaper had succumbed to Alzheimer's, and this opportunity too was closed down. It was a bad time for Töst. *The Absence of Real Desire* was a film he felt good about and thought should be better regarded. *Screw* magazine reviewed it favourably, but with an interesting caveat: 'The photography is classy, the cast attractive, the sex is outstanding and the black and white inserts gratifyingly sleazy. That's the problem. Unless you leave your brains behind, this movie could get your hand off your cock because it makes you think.'

The review did have a positive outcome. An old acquaintance from Copenhagen days, now something of a leading pornography distributor, was in New York and read the review. As a result Töst was able to sell European rights. It netted him less than he would have liked. Sloppy drafting of the agreement with Nussbaum and the Californians made international title problematic. As Töst himself put it: 'If I couldn't do heavy, I could do pathetic. These were not bad people, I had made them money, and in any case, this was peripheral to their main source of revenue. To be nice made them feel good and was affordable, but don't be fooled, nice was just this side of mean.'

Nonetheless, there was enough to keep Töst going. He began to rebuild contacts in the business. There was a lot of work. His reputation was, on balance, very positive. He had come to recognise, however, that pornography was going corporate. Competent routine performances from actors to a format and a budget were the only output. It was also where he had started years before in Soho. Whatever the brief flirtation the bourgeoisie had enjoyed with Pornography as Art in Manhattan cinemas and private homes, the real revenue was still in the hands of sweaty men in small and dingy auditoriums; and video was on its way.

In the ensuing months, Töst attempted to get to grips with the new conditions. Not yet forty, he felt he had become irrelevant. His vision of sexual explicitness had been bifurcated into anodyne romanticism or continued crude sexploitation at the lowest level. He contacted Louis Bates in order to discover whether there were any monies left in the Trust that the ever-thoughtful, if increasingly disenchanted, Bates had established. There were, and these were transferred to Töst's account in

Manhattan. Töst also recognised that he was starting to drink too heavily again.

Life in Greenwich Village in the early 1970s could be pleasing enough. There were good bars, cheap eateries and compatible people to meet. That said, for both Bernd and Dwight, good friends as they were, just for a houseguest, as he had become, to commute to Manhattan and return drunk was not satisfactory. Mrs Brimley, who was very fond of 'Bernie', said: 'I liked him. He was a gentleman even when drunk. I was just never sure how useful it was to have a celebrity in our home. I stayed awake wondering if he had fallen off the ferry.' Dwight himself had segued his role and connections from the Stampetti family into a lucrative limousine business and moved to Staten Island.

The outcome was that Bernd went south to the sun in the early Fall of 1972. Through a contact of Dwight's, he had, at very cheap rental, a substantial trailer in an Adult Holiday and Retirement Park by the Suwannee River in Florida, not far from the Georgia border.

Sunshine apart, Töst also used alcohol as part of his retreat from reality. He was an orderly and inoffensive drunk, mostly sitting outside his trailer drinking scotch. Once or twice a week he borrowed a neighbour's pick-up and drove to a bar in the town. The local police had become used to his habits and respected his controlled behaviour more than they cared about the probability he was well over the limit for a DUI.

In the following Spring he decided to return to New York. He rang Dwight to check whether he could come and stay. His friend said of course, then warned Töst that the IRS wanted to see him in relation to various taxation issues. The investigation was only in part about unpaid tax from Töst's own income.

Of considerably greater interest was the Stampetti business empire in particular, and the porn business in general. Töst admits he took the easiest way out. In return for immunity, and the lightest of back payment penalties, he told the IRS everything he knew about the way the business had worked. This did not make him any friends and Dwight warned him that New York was not a good place for Töst to stay. Brimley himself had mixed feelings. He had long ceased to work for the Stampettis but retained a regard for the family and a distaste for finks. On the other hand, Töst had become a friend and Dwight understood the motivation to avoid jail. Toward the end of the Summer of 1973 the IRS returned Töst's passport and he left for Amsterdam, having borrowed the airfare from Dwight.

In Amsterdam it was relatively easy to find work making pornographic shorts. Censorship was effectively over and video was improving all the time, though still evolving in terms of the systems; the main struggle being between VHS and Betamax. Töst did not like video, but could see its advantages. He preferred Betamax for its then superior technical and professional qualities, even though he soon realised that home viewing – and VHS porn – was the future. Which it was for the next two decades. The money was not very good, but it provided a living and he was able to repay Dwight's loan. He was also able to rebuild contacts in Holland, Germany and Denmark, in all of which countries he still had a good reputation as a pioneer – indeed, almost grand old man.

In the Autumn of 1974, he was in Hamburg filming a one-hour sex film, which was essentially a series of promiscuous encounters between two girls and various men. He was surprised and impressed by one of the girls, a young woman called Sonja. Töst remarked of her: 'She was attractive enough, nice body and so on, but not beautiful. But she was incredibly sexy. I mean, she reeked sex, loved it, wanted it badly, could not get enough. I tell you, most times in my experience the women will get some fun out of the sex – they rarely do movies if they don't enjoy it to a point. At worst, they'll like one of the studs and tolerate the rest. Sonja was the only one I've come across who truly lived for fucking. Not only that, she loved being fucked everywhere, and she loved taking several men on simultaneously. For the first time ever, I got an erection when filming because she was so sexual. She exuded a hot oestrogen scent.'

After the movie was finished Töst met the distributor – a seriously rich German who owned one of Europe's leading pornographic labels. Töst mentioned how impressed he was with Sonja. The distributor agreed and, over a drink with the three of them, commissioned them to produce a feature with Sonja as a star. Töst recalled: 'He told me he thought the combination of my reputation and her sexiness would make a strong commercial pitch to the market. He also told me not to get too fancy. He said this is sex, not art. He did let me use 16mm – though it had to be colour. That was fine with me. I did use black and white for the title intro and dressed the set and lit everything so it felt a bit Otto Dix.'

The idea for *The Sick Room* came from a conversation between Töst and Sonja. They were catching up on their sex life histories and Töst mentioned his experience with Noreen. Sonja was thrilled and suggested they make a film about exactly that. Töst said: 'She told me that one of her fantasies had been – was still – to be in a boys' school, or a college or something and fuck all the fellows there. I told her to come back with her best fantasies. I was most interested in how I created something distinctive in atmosphere.'

Töst met Ralph Farebrother in a bar in Hamburg. Ralph himself has very clear memories of the time and the events surrounding the film. He told me: 'I was working in this bar – quite a smart place, but something of a rendezvous for tarts and businessmen. To be honest, I had a sideline as a gigolo when the opportunity occurred. Hamburg may seem an odd place to practise that profession but, you know, I rather fancied German women and there was a surprising number of frustrated, rich Hausfraus there. Anyway, Töst appeared in my life and after a couple of visits to the bar we got into conversation and he asked if I would be interested in making this film. I didn't say this in our little group get-together but, I tell you, when I met Sonja, I was knocked out. She was sex on wheels, old boy. So I counted myself in.'

Ralph apart, assembling the cast was primarily Sonja's valuable contribution. It must also be admitted that the schoolboy element involved a certain amount of suspended disbelief. As Töst put it: 'The so-called boys were as much like adolescents as the cast of *Grease*.' Nonetheless, at Töst's insistence, the younger men in the cast had to shed their adult mid-seventies look. They cut their hair and lost their moustaches and even shaved their legs. Töst didn't want the Hispanic look so the feel was Nordic. Ralph recalls that Sonja endorsed the hairiness taboo and rather enjoyed bullying the actors into submission. The older 'schoolmasters' were recruited from a swingers group, and the Wagnerian matron from a fetish club.

This character was entirely Sonja's idea and Töst remembers her saying enthusiastically: 'I always wanted to be fucked in the ass by a dyke with a dildo.' It transpired the 'matron' didn't like sex a lot, but was very happy to wield whips and implements.

Töst had some mixed feelings about this movie. He felt he had compromised a certain rigour of vision for simple erotic indulgence. Nonetheless, he was pleased with the way he had taken the raw narrative of porn video and combined it with some perceptual depth and the visual richness of film. He liked the manner in which the central pair, Sonja and Ralph, established a quite distinctive dramatic relationship so that the melee of actors – in fact half a dozen – appeared as ciphers, except for the matron, who acted as a ring-mistress for the central duo and supporting cast. Most of all, Töst was gratified by a reviewer at the Frankfurt Erotic Film Festival who wrote: 'The work is an intriguing combination of Shakespeare and Brecht as the couple enact their passion on a completely different mental plane from the rest of the action. All the other sexual activities are merely fantasies – admittedly among the most libidinous over which I have come unaided, in my underwear.'

The distributor was pleased with the quality and glad to pay Töst a worthwhile fee for his direction. He used the film – and Sonja – as a promotional tool for his entire label. In its own right, it sold well; in a later video transfer even better. It left Töst in good standing with the business. The problem was that by 1975 a new generation of pornographic film and filmmakers had begun to take control. It was about video – anyone could do it – the audiences were increasingly home audiences. Directors, however well respected in the trade, were unnecessary. As was later to happen to photographers everywhere in all media with the advent of the digital camera

– fast and cheap were the only criteria, and any edit problems could be fixed on the computer. The concept of narrative was at best deconstructed, if not irrelevant. (See Appendix 3).

Chapter 4
The Last Reel, 1975 – 2003

Töst himself observed: 'It was a time when the business was just going for volume. I had no problem with it being single-minded on sex, but there was no fun, no style. Later I think some kind of enjoyment and quality got back in, especially in the States. Nothing great, but the girls got more confident and took charge, to some extent, of their performances. Back then it was a bleak time with only three directorial instructions – get it up, get it in, squirt it out. I guess it hasn't changed in that, really. Hollywood and the straight movie business keeps peeking over the border fence but of course they're stymied. Everything and anything can be done except the one slam dunk moment when the boys and girls give each other the juice in full view. Why we want to watch that eludes me, but we do. Maybe we want to see something we don't often look at, or need to recapture; maybe it's some kind of primal thing – we need to watch sex and death because we understand about consciousness of self and mortality. I think this terrifies us as a society. It is too deep to contemplate. I think women seem to need it less than do men because so much is inside them already, but what do I know? So, be that as it may, video made sex a fast food empire. That is, you take stuff that is intrinsically worthwhile and scrummy and good for you and use technology to turn it into total crap. When I photographed a cock or a cunt or whatever combination of bits I truly did want to say, "Look at this. It is so sexy and such fun. Look at what is happening here." It's true that often my work would suggest the downside. The fear and loathing, to borrow a phrase. That's because humans subvert so many things of value, and that's because we either simply miss the point – like with religion – or because we overdose on some ingredient – like drugs or sex. So, for many reasons, most still a mystery to me, I couldn't just do pretty, like Elvira Madigan. Sex isn't pretty to watch anyway; it is beautiful in the way a tiger killing a deer is beautiful, or giving birth. The close-up is only pretty in our heads and if we are in love or lust. Oddly, male gay films have a kind of erotic integrity; they are one hundred per cent high-octane dirty fucking. I don't get turned on by it, though I know many women do, but I do respect how the guys just go at it. Sonja was one of the few women who had that rawness in her approach to fucking.'

Töst spent the next three years moving between Hamburg, Copenhagen and Amsterdam. On his own admission he earned his living alongside tyro camera managers in the production of endless video representations of the sexual act, mostly involving multiple partners. Töst was not proud of this period. 'Frankly, I felt a better human being in the trailer in Suwannee,' he said. He did take comfort from his refusal – as, still, a director of reputation – to film what he described as 'the totally gross freak-out stuff those sleaze-bags wanted at times'. Fortunately, extreme markets were just that and Töst was able to exercise discretion over the material he filmed. He particularly recalled a period when the use of stills and out-takes also fuelled the printed pornography market. 'I chose the angles for these guys and lit well, shot pin-sharp so they could reprint. It got me work, just like my ability from way back to shoot segments. You know, at this time I suddenly realised I was like all those good babes like Julie, Lorraine, Rosita,

Helga, Sonja and Cayman. A whore, in truth, but with an idea about things having a point and being done right. This made it easier for a while until, like them, I thought that getting fucked was not enough.' (See Appendix 5).

In 1979, Töst decided to return, if possible, to America, his resident alien's visa having lapsed. Much to his surprise, the authorities seemed to have no problem renewing. Whether it was simply an inattentive embassy in Paris – where his French passport required him to apply – or, as he believes, the IRS wanting him more easily available for questioning will never be known. He re-entered the USA via New York, and returned to the Brimley household. Before doing so, he recorded an abortive programme with Edna Weiskopf, for *Arena*, in London (see appendix 4). Twenty years later, that encounter still made him laugh. 'What they didn't record was, as we left the studio, I asked her if it would help if I gave her oral sex. Luckily for me, she opined that violent death would be preferable. I think she meant for both of us.'

Most of the pornographic film work, and certainly anything with a pretension to some kind of quality, had long since moved to California. Töst, however, had grown tired of making sex films and rather liked life in Manhattan: except for the winters. He therefore resolved to spend half the year, from late Spring to Fall, in New York and the other half in Los Angeles. He also needed work; never very careful with money, his funds were low. Dwight said he had considered offering Töst a job as a chauffeur. That Töst had no valid US or, it transpired, driver's licence of any sort proved a crucial obstacle. Töst himself was perfectly insouciant about the matter. 'I never drove that much, never rented a car, never crashed. I certainly didn't want to drive limos for Dwight. I'd have cleaned his shoes, and did, but not drive his vehicles.'

With an introduction from Dwight, Töst found a job as manager-caretaker in a run-down tourist hotel on the West Side, near the north end of Central Park. There was not much to do. The coffee shop was franchised out and the few staff knew their jobs. Administration was a straightforward routine. The hotel depended in the Summer on tourists, mostly Europeans, on cheap week or long-weekend packages. Interwoven with the tourists, and important for the off-season, were the hookers and their clients. It was this clientele that gave Töst his reason for being employed. His salary was minimal and therefore in need of supplementing. His job was to manage the bookings so that occupancy at rack rent was maximised. Judicious selection of commercial partners – especially those who only needed a very short let – could ensure rooms being sold at two or three times their theoretical daily rack rent. On occasion this might even involve using a tourist room in the absence of their official guests. Töst proved adept in this role and earned decent cash commissions, as was expected by his employers. He was, after all, drawing on a lifetime experience of the underground economy. His IRS liaison had been either forgotten or forgiven by the underworld. This in itself suggests he had not transgressed too badly.

Whatever was the case, Töst earned a solid if modest living, the hotel gave its owners an income, and the hookers had a secure base. It may even be imagined that the clients had a good time. Dwight refused to discuss details of the situation. He said: 'Man, everybody was happy. I tell you, in another world, Bernie could have managed the Plaza. He had this knack of cosying up without being sycophantic, you know. In five minutes folk would be doing anything he asked. Plus, and this is central, he was efficient. Man, he came across laid-back, but on the detail! Well, that's why he was a good film director.'

Since Töst rather enjoyed his work – reminiscent in some ways, he once commented, of his early days in Paris and London, he tended to live at the hotel, thus relieving the Brimley ménage from its houseguest.

His old circle of acquaintances, business associates and film world people had become somewhat attenuated over the years. However, the fact that he had produced a considerable output, albeit some films more distinguished in quality than others, ensured his ongoing currency in the circles where these things were relevant. Sadly, the circles in question had contracted somewhat from quite a broad sweep around central Manhattan to a more constricted enclave based on the conjunction of 42nd Street and Times Square. Nonetheless, there were still bars and restaurants of character where ongoing players and respected survivors could meet and reminisce or even dream dreams.

That winter he took a train to Los Angeles, stopping off at various points on the way. Mostly, he said, to get drunk for a couple of days, but also because he felt he had not seen enough of his adopted country. In LA he rented an efficiency just off La Brea, and not far from Woloshin's delicatessen. There, he became a regular and after a few weeks took a job as a counter hand. His linguistic abilities – fluent German, competent Polish especially – commended him to the manager. The wage, though small, was adequate for rent, drink and groceries and the winter passed pleasantly.

For the ensuing four or five years, Töst lived in quiet obscurity, his alternating winter and summer residences and occupations accepted by his employers and enjoyed by Töst. He said of that period: 'In many ways it was one of my happiest times. There was no stress, the folk I worked with were congenial, I hardly saw rain or felt cold. What's more, I thought very little about sex. Once in a while I would dream about some sexy girl sitting on my face and pumping my cock, or simply a good straight fuck, but it was no big deal to do without real physical sex. It was a perfect dropout life – almost Zen in its simplicity.'

Then, in the Spring of 1985, Töst received via Dwight, courtesy of the organiser's persistence and ingenuity in the use of databases, an expenses-paid trip to Japan to be a guest of honour at an alternative film festival. *Fick Alles* had received an award. Töst recalled: 'I'd never really thought much about the Japs, you know. Suddenly there's this first-class air ticket and these really polite short people being incredibly nice to me. I had no idea I was so big over there. Of course, there is quite a crowd of Western film people of varying legitimacy, and some flaky straight actors – including a few big names – who are doing the sex as art bullshit at a safe distance from their home circuit. Still, it's a fun-packed few days. The bonus was to meet up with Sonja and Helga. Helga, of course, was in the business running clubs or something. She looked good though and we had a few cocktails together. Sonja was still incredibly sexy and I had my first fuck in three years. In fact, I had several fucks. She was outstanding in the sack; I think she was the one who did the fucking. I couldn't believe I'd never fucked her when we were making the film. How self-controlled is that! Anyway, it turns out Sonja is now running a chain of sex boutiques and is stinking rich. I think she and Helga did a deal of some sort.'

The meeting with Sonja led to a film commission. She had in mind that Töst should direct a series of what she called 'Beautiful People Unplugged'. Her concept was a series of explicit sex videos that would appeal to the more mainstream and often female audience for 'naughty but nice' who frequented her boutiques. The 'casting' would replicate, if not draw on, that pool of actors and models who populate ads, lifestyle TV series and softcore movies. Töst was dubious about the project. He was aware and quite cynical about the reality that many actors had undertaken somewhat risqué work at some point in their career – if then not quite so egregiously as Pamela Anderson had subsequently, albeit in an apparent home movie, and later still, Paris Hilton. In that respect there was no problem. 'The bizarre twist in this was that whereas actors often make a big deal about body doubles, in this project I sometimes had to find face doubles.' His main concern was to do with what he described as 'that strange three-step process that gets us from racy through soft to hardcore'.

Töst returned to LA, with money in his bank account from Sonja, to try and put the project together. He did not regard it as an especially happy period. His regard for and sense of obligation to Sonja was great. His empathy with the idea was minimal. He could understand what his producer was looking for, and he felt perfectly able to deliver it. It was just that it was not the sort of film he made.

In a letter to Sonja, which followed her visit to LA to view the cuts and approve the final version of the tape, Töst wrote,

'I'm glad you liked the movie. It is certainly as pretty as it can get on video. I find it hard to tell you why I find the concept so difficult. Cunts and cocks are not pretty, but earthy. Some are more aesthetic than others, but either people are turned on by seeing them in action or they're not. The scrotum in soft focus is just that. I do understand and respect what you are trying to do. Even so, if you want to turn nice bourgeois ladies and men onto sex, I think you would do better to make movies of modern ballroom dancing – especially the Latin section. You should watch it on British TV. I think you will find enough material in my tapes for at least three sixty-minute videos properly edited. There is some change left from your generous payment so let me know where to send it. Thanks, babe, for everything. Big love, best wishes, B.'

This was the end of the project. Sonja more than recouped her investment in it, through the shops, although she was rather disappointed in the sales, and Töst's critique was, if not vindicated, given some validity. She never reclaimed the underspending on her investment, nor did she ask Töst to do any further work. Their relationship remained cordial and they exchanged annual greetings until Töst died.

Sonja was courteous enough to meet me for a drink on a visit to England. Having established that my intentions toward Töst were honourable, she not only talked at length about him, but gave me a bundle of his greetings cards and occasional letters.

'I just liked him a great deal,' she said. 'He could be very funny, and he sort of had an ideal concept of women. He made us feel well regarded. I think this came from his upbringing. Don't get me wrong, he was certainly a proper male and I think he struggled with his emotional instincts and physical feelings. This is why his movies are, shall we say, slightly strange. Maybe I shouldn't tell you this, but it is part of his character. I think you know I was pretty damn sex-mad. He was very correct when we made our film. Then, after we met again, I loved him because he was so relaxed in bed. There were no conflicts; he just let me sort of decide. So we fucked when I wanted some comfort, not just when I was horny. We enjoyed each other very well. You know, he was so right about the ballroom dancing thing. I still find it quite erotic to watch. Bernd said it was the first sign of age.'

His excursion to Japan and the subsequent filmmaking had somewhat fractured Töst's connections stateside. He remained close to Dwight but the hotel job had gone, as had his post at Woloshin's. Even though he had felt uncomfortable making Sonja's movies, the experience of the Japan film festival and working for her had rekindled his interest in film. It had also renewed his reputation. In consequence, and as is the way of things, one day Syd knocked on the door of Töst's apartment. He explained that he had planned and contracted to make a new TV soap series that aimed to sail not only as close to the law as was allowed on network TV – which was not very far – but that would have an uncensored version for cable. He recommended an actor who had featured in Sonja's video who had also mentioned Töst as a 'very good guy' and had given him Töst's address. Töst's only comment in reference to the actor on this introduction was to remark, 'He was just a soft focus prick to me.' Nonetheless, Töst needed the money and became, in effect, a second unit director, filming as before the up, in and away sequences with which he had begun his career.

After the pilot and three episodes, the studio folded the series. Audiences were not favourable and the adult version frightened the lawyers. Töst had shot a considerable number of inserts and he was not sure what to do with them. Syd told him to hang on to the material and he would sort something out – this, because Töst had seen little money for his efforts. Some weeks later, two tall men in dark suits called at Töst's apartment and, opening an attaché case that contained several bundles of dollar bills, requested the film material. As Töst put it: 'It seemed foolish to count the money or ask any questions. We parted without violence being an issue. I never did find out the whys and wherefores of the deal.'

Restored to reasonable fiscal liquidity, Töst took himself on holiday to Mexico. He rented a small beach house on the Gulf coast and enjoyed three or four months of peaceful nothingness. He recalled: 'I think it was then that I really started to slide. The relaxation bit was a delusion. There was nothing to do except lie around and drink and look at the sea. There were a few of us gringos around and we'd get together in a bar or someone's house and do what? Get drunk is what. Or I would go to some local cantina that was full of Mexicans also getting drunk. It was the drunkest place I've ever been. If I had stayed sober, I would have had a problem about sex. There was one fat whore in town, but a lot of very pretty señoritas desperate to fuck an Americano. It is obvious why that might be so; it's the same everywhere you have rich men and poor women. The problem was that these chicks had fathers and boyfriends, and the guys carried knives, if not guns. It is pretty lonely down by the beach, so I made sure it stayed that way.'

Töst recounted how once, a girl appeared at his house and was more than blatant in her effort to seduce him. He sent her away as politely as he could. The next day, a villager appeared and presented him with a chicken. It was, he explained, because the gringo had been an honourable man and had not defiled the honour of the girl or her family. 'We know,' said the man, 'because we were watching from the trees. But if you want her, it can be arranged.' Töst had no ambitions to acquire a Mexican family, and explained he was otherwise committed. The precise nature of these obligations he left unspecified. 'It was either that I was already married or a homosexual,' he said. 'Their take out was their problem.'

'Eventually,' said Töst, 'it got so I was hardly sober from breakfast on. I had tried to write but had nothing much to say that I thought worth saying. Then the money was getting low, so I headed back to LA.' Dwight commented that money had not just got low but had vanished completely, and that Töst had called him collect to ask for a loan to get him out of Mexico. Back in his efficiency off La Brea, Töst found a letter from Hollywood Personal Services Inc. Its chief operating officer was called Rumer L. Tissick. He wondered if Mr Töst, whose reputation for discretion and technical competence in film had been vouched for, would be interested in discussion of a business proposition. Though the letter was some weeks old, Töst called and was given an appointment.

'I turned up sober and tanned,' said Töst. 'This Tissick was middle-aged, very smooth. I think he was Austrian by ancestry at least and when he found my German was fluent and socially acceptable, we got on well. Anyway, among other things, his company did surveillance and divorce work and that sort of stuff. They'd latched on to the power of video and he wants a good man with a camera. I point out that it's no big deal to point a video camera out of a car window and I'm a film director. He goes ho hum, yes, but it's not so straightforward as that and I was specially recommended. Well, by now it is nearly midday and I have yet to have a drink so I am getting irritable. Then Tissick says the sort of work I would have to do involves not just the film thing but editing it and making sure it looks good. To cut it short, the job is actually to film very personal group-sex things and general carrying-on for rich clients who like to review their sex lives and possibly share them with others.

'The funny thing was I was quite shocked. I mean it sounded like the plot for a movie. I think I had got out of touch with real life over the years. This was perfectly logical, totally sound thinking, the ultimate in home movies. Naturally, I said yes.'

Until the early 1990s Töst enjoyed modest, if closet, success as the director of choice for the dissolute rich. He confessed himself astonished at the scope of his new trade. 'First, you would be blown away if you knew whom of the rich and famous lead these really abandoned lives. I mean, way beyond the scandal sheet innuendos. Second, you would probably be a tad depressed if you saw some of the casualties – the betrayed, the drug dependent; the abused, frankly. Third, you would have something of a laugh at how ridiculous people can be. I know my job was always about sex, but with these folk, believe me, it restored my faith in professionals. Don't mistake me, I'm comfortable with people doing whatever. If you want to photograph your lover's fat ass crapping, or record your premature ejaculation, please do; it's your privilege and, hopefully, good for your relationship. My own issue was just with these rich shitty people: it was like the last days of the Roman Republic. Be that as it may, I earned some good money, got to visit some high-tone places and learned a great deal about what goes on at the country club. I also saw some very fine bodies and some much less fine than you would have thought, and witnessed some scenes that would get me very rich, if they didn't get me dead first. I mean, this was Rolls-Royce *Gonzo*. There seemed to be any number of pretty Mexican garden boys looking after the gay producers and Hispanic gigolos servicing the ageing divas. Then there was very widespread fetish, bondage and the regular thwack of leather on flesh. The blackmail potential was huge. I was offered hundreds of thousands by some of the professionals who took part to slip them a print: not a chance, compadre, these folk had protection.'

The deal with Tissick and HPS Inc. was simple. For a small monthly retainer plus per diems, Töst would be on call to provide a video record of whatever proceedings a client requested, fully processed and edited to the client's satisfaction. HPS Inc. would bill all costs and fees to the client. Töst would be entitled to retain any cash or other emoluments the grateful client chose to offer. Whilst he was able to move from his modest efficiency to a decent apartment not too far from the Beverly Hills Hotel, which was his unofficial office-rendezvous, Töst still had to be careful with money.

In our last conversations, Töst described this time as his 'Indian Summer'. By 1992, the events of the first Gulf War had set a new tone. The sex industry ploughed on, and there was no doubt that the rich and debauched continued to fuck, and drug themselves indulgently. That said, HPS Inc. found itself with a declining business in the commissioned sex video sector. In part, Töst thought, this was simply because there were fewer players. People were becoming more serious-minded and politically correct. Some of the protagonists were too old or even dead. He also perceived that technology made it ever more easy to adopt a DIY approach to home recording of however sophisticated a nature. Töst said: 'Tissick was too old, I was too old. Some celebrities showed publicly that you could do it yourself, which everyone knew anyway. It was just a craze for a specific generation. Plus we would never touch the truly heavy areas of torture-type things and serious underage. And, trust me, there was some of that, though not on my watch. I told the Grand Jury I'd heard stories, but never seen it. I think Tissick was an OK guy. If folk get off on dressing up like Lolita, or some heavy S&M, that's fine; but the other things, not for me. Plus Tissick gave me carte blanche to pull the plug if I thought what was going on was likely to cause us trouble. Except drugs. Without drugs most of those guys couldn't operate anyway.'

When asked for specific incidents in his experience as pornographer to the stars, Töst remained reticent. 'I got paid to do a job, and that included a tight mouth,' he said. 'Overall, it was much as you might imagine. Beautiful people – up to a point, as I said, since they owe a lot to cosmetics and surgery – but to be fair they are often still quite well put together. I was able to be quiet and let them get on with their lives. What would you expect – pools, cocktails, one or two very well-trusted and well-paid staff, some charades and costumes.

I mean, in the end it was just about people who liked to play sex games getting their rocks off and who had the cash to give it a setting and keep a record.'

He was also shy of his reference to the casualties. 'Look at it this way. There were some real grown-up ladies who had made choices, which may or may not have worked. There were some bimbos who decided they could make a career on their backs. There were a lot of pros in this and quite a few of the clients were voyeurs. There were surprising numbers of men who wanted to watch their wives get it, and wives who liked watching gays go to it. Sometimes they'd give themselves a bit-part. You don't always have friends to play like that. I can see that this is about whether men or women call the shots – but to quote a well-known movie, "I don't give a damn". We all of us do what we do. There were bullies and sad sacks from all sexes.'

In 1993, just as he was about to return to New York, Töst received a subpoena to give evidence at the Grand Jury indictment of his former employer, Rumer L. Tissick. The charges were multiple and included procurement of minors for immoral purposes, drug trafficking and solicitation of obscene acts. In an interview with the prosecuting District Attorney, it was made clear to Töst that he was expected to be a co-operative witness unless he wanted to end up in the dock as well.

'To me that was no contest,' said Töst. 'I had no knowledge of what lay behind the charges so could say nothing damaging. All I had to do was tell it like it was.' The transcript of his main evidence is printed in full in Appendix 6. Töst says he quite enjoyed his day in court. The brouhaha also benefited him in that *Confidential* magazine and several European scandal sheets offered him considerable sums to tell his story, and to hand over any tapes he might still have in his possession. He confessed to me that he had played chicken on the whole matter. Whilst the money would have been welcome, he feared that the sanctions from offended parties could have been severe in the extreme. In the event, although two or three personalities had their reputations damaged and some careers were put on hold, various deals and legal finagling prevented very much from being aired. The charges against Tissick were dropped. Töst once again found himself in receipt of a visit by dark-suited men with an attaché case containing money. This time the message was explicit: 'This is for being a good boy. Keep it that way.'

On the downside, the case had pretty well obliterated Töst's reputation as having been an interesting director of curious films about sex. He was forever in Hollywood's canyons and canons as that home-porn moviemaker who nearly went down to a Grand Jury. He hung around the area for another year until the money ran out, the barmen and their customers grew tired of him and he was forced to retreat to the Brimley home on Staten Island for a brief period. He said himself: 'I was a pain in the ass to everyone, whining and getting drunk and shooting my mouth off. I hated me, and so did everyone else.' Scraping together what funds he could, Bernd headed back to LA.

Much later, as we reviewed the typescript of this biography in our one, week-long meeting in New Hampshire, Töst laid down the pages and sighed. 'I did one hell of a job in that testimony. I earned the cheap pay-off they gave me. Like I told you before, it wasn't the bimbos and wannabes. Yes, there were the girls doing all styles of sex without a lot of pleasure, but they had an aim and were aware of the price. Worse, though, were the private videos where couples were really giving each other a hard time. They were involved in some ritual of lust and hate and dependency. I don't know where this puts me in sexual politics but I shot stuff where the woman was the dominant partner and others where the man was. The latter gave me an occasional problem. I could never get used to the idea of a woman being abused or, let's say, used against her will. There was a lot of that, believe me, inevitably focused on sodomy and whips and chains – the whole bondage schtick and so forth. Some women had a thing for it, many clearly did not. On the other hand, there were those men who seemed to like being generally put down and mauled, and literally pissed on and even crapped on by their women. Including one or two surprisingly well-known, macho types. For me this was no problem. I liked watching strong women in action.' Töst sat back and laughed. 'Don't kid yourself, pain is not my thing. I have gone years without sex because I can think about it and because several hundred gallons of cheap liquor, even if they undermine the performance, sharpen the imaginative desires.'

What was to be the final decade of Töst's life was not one he cared to reminisce about. Increasingly financially precarious and dependent on alcohol, he relied on subsidies from Dwight and one or two other friends, supplemented by the odd bit of casual work in the sex industry. At first this had at least been technical, involving editing or even camera work.

Toward the end of the 1990s, however, he was reduced to the management of an adult video and magazine store in Bay City. The job itself only materialised courtesy of the owner, whom Töst had met in a bar and who had known and liked his work. Dwight was reluctant to admit it, but he had himself bought a small condo apartment near Bernd's beloved Woloshin's, which he pretended was owned by an old business partner of the Stampetti family, and therefore on offer to Töst rent-free. 'It was nothing,' he said. 'Just a property investment.'

As this book progressed, it became increasingly important to me that the subject and I met and spent some time together. Our relationship had gone well and we communicated frequently and as friends. I sent him as often as I could drafts of the text, which he would usually send back quite promptly. Delays or awkwardness could be attributed to his hangovers or general depression. In the last year of his life, undoubtedly his diagnosed terminal illness – liver failure – must have been a major factor. It is in retrospect astonishing that he was so generally amiable.

In the Summer of 2002, I was fortunate to have the offer of a house in New Hampshire for the Fall. I mentioned this to Töst, in one of our long telephone conversations. He immediately said, 'Oh, lucky you, I've never seen the Fall in New England.' My spontaneous invitation was accepted – as was the promise of an air ticket, which is how, early in October of that year, I found myself standing in the arrivals terminal of our tiny commuter airport, waiting for Bernd's plane to arrive.

His black eyepatch, straggly short beard, and the Slavic cheekbones he inherited – as did Minou – from his mother were unmistakable. He was very genial, probably slightly squiffy and, despite his buoyant manner, declared as ill by his gaunt and jaundiced complexion. We hugged. He took my wife's hand and stooped over it with great Germanic courtesy. 'It is a great pleasure to meet not only my biographer, but his very beautiful wife of whom he speaks too little.' The performance was pure ham. But it was very good ham. Töst had the ability to adopt the language and intonations that suited the moment. For this moment he was the exotic, European mongrel, film genius. My wife, who had expressed some reservations about using a week of our vacation on this 'deadbeat pornographer', as she described him, was successfully disarmed.

For the next five days, we alternated short walks around the local lake with long car excursions through the autumnal forests of this most civilised State of the Union. Töst sat in the back seat and sighed as each mountain and valley landscape, each perfectly constructed township, was revealed. 'You know, maman and Minou would have loved to live here. This is as good as Northern Hemisphere civilisation gets.' Through the evenings, we reviewed the typescript of this book and, with the aid of a taperecorder, added more material, much of which has been incorporated in the narrative. Töst enjoyed talking with the tape on, especially when a couple of Martinis had made him loquacious and unselfconscious. He liked less the process of reviewing written material. At one point, when I had left him with the text of the early chapters, he came into the living room and threw it down carelessly. 'Look, I expect this is fine. I trust you. In any case, who is going to sue whom if you've got it wrong?'

Toward the end of his visit, I took courage to ask him once more about Minou. His response was unequivocal. He said, 'I've told you as much as I am able to or want to. It may be other people have stuff to add. Ask Louis. You know how I felt, and still feel, about Minou. To go back is not an option.' Later, over the remnants of a bottle of Scotch, and after a reflective moonlit walk along the lakeshore, he said: 'I think you should get a copy of the typescript to my sister. She has to approve it.' I asked him if he wanted this confirmed in writing. He answered as before: 'It's a trust thing. There isn't time to sue people.' This was the only time he alluded to his awareness of a foreseeable death. I did not pursue the topic, nor attempt in any way to deter him from taking his own route out. When he fell asleep in his chair, I covered him with a rug and left him. He appeared late the following morning, looking no different – that is, just as raddled – but carrying a bundle of bedding. 'Sorry,' he said. 'Scotch is too good a soporific, so I wet the bed.' His matter-of-fact and wholly relaxed attitude made the incident entirely unremarkable. It was as if that was what guests might do after a long evening. Somehow, it made his skill as a director and ability to survive clearer. I saw why Dwight Brimley, and the actors who had worked for him, spoke so kindly of him. There was no pretence.

The day before his departure, we drove to Hanover to see the famous Dartmouth University campus there. As we strolled along the tranquil, very beautiful, colonial streets, Töst said, in reference to the previous year's catastrophe: 'Isn't it crazy that a culture that can create this and espouse such fine principles should also generate such hatred?' Then suddenly the streets became populated by students bustling from their classes. It was noon. We watched them: they were much like students everywhere. 'It is a great pity,' said Töst, 'that we still can't manage to make love rather than war.' He turned to my wife and me and grinned, as if conscious that he was in danger of being trite. 'Though we have to remember, in western male parlance, that to fuck is also to break something or someone, and, or, generally place at a serious disadvantage.'

His last evening we spent quietly at home in our house in the forest by the lake. Töst drank remarkably little. Our conversation was comfortably fragmented and general. I knew he had shut up shop on recollections. I mentioned some matters regarding the timetable for final texts and approvals. He smiled and gave a shrug: 'Whenever.' Then he leaned forward and, smiling quite kindly into my eyes, said: 'I find it ironic that it should be an Englishman who has chosen to write my epitaph. Though I still think you are a renegade Jew. It is stuff like this that helps me to figure out how you Brits got to be so big in the world. Though I still don't really understand it.'

The following day we drove to Boston. Töst had decided he would like to go back through New York and spend some days with Dwight. We left him at the train station – flying was his least preferred mode of travel. He shook hands with me, kissed my wife on both cheeks and said he had had a good time and was happy with the way things had worked out. Then he picked up his single, scuffed valise, turned away and walked through the portico toward the Amtrak booking office.

After my return to England, Dwight called me. He was affable and wished only to say that 'Bernie' had arrived in good shape and had given a positive report of both the social and business side of his stay. 'I think this was real good for him,' added Dwight. 'Thank you for that.' Töst had stayed for a few days and then taken the train back to LA and his apartment. I said I thought Töst looked unwell. Dwight was quiet for a moment, then he said: 'Yeah, if I were you, I'd push the peanut forward quite fast.'

The commission to gain Minou's approval was now the major hurdle to publication. I very much wanted her consent before Töst died. Naturally, it was to Louis Bates that I turned. Despite his age and expressed disenchantment with the Tösts, he had too long and too close a connection to sever completely. He agreed to write to Minou – he felt email would lack proper dignity – enclosing the draft so far and let me know. A reply came more promptly than we had expected. Minou gave her approval to the text and had no comments to make. She hoped that we would let 'BB' know she loved him, and was well,and happy. She would like it if her children could meet their uncle, but respected his feelings. She ignored a request to meet personally with her.

The typescript was now print-, or rather proof-ready when Louis received an email from Minou. She would be in Paris the following week and wished to see me. Of course, the invitation could not be refused.

The woman who walked over to me in the reception of the George V was quite different to my imagined Minou. The gamine that I, and probably Bernd, had held in our perceptions or memories was now a stylish French matron. For women to be always described by their physical appearance is a modern concern of manners. Minou, though stockier than I had supposed, was illumined by an extraordinary, wide smile and dark, thoughtful eyes. In other respects she was perfectly coiffured and clad in the way one would expect of a French chatelaine in her fifties. I greeted her as restrainedly as I could, given my eagerness and knowledge. She accepted my compliments and suggested we go to the cocktail bar. It was a short, very civilised and rather moving thirty minutes or so. Minou had worked out what she wanted to say, and she was, like her brother, adamant about further questions. In as faithful a record as my feeble shorthand could manage – she refused a tape recorder – this is what she said in her correct and formal English:

'I want it made clear how much I love and owe to my brother. Our sexual relationship will be of prurient interest to many. I can say, quite clearly, that my whole time with Bernd was my salvation and my anchor. Of course it was about sex – we were young – but it was also about love and emotions. He and I needed each other and were, above all, best friends. I have no shame or regret. It ended because I found someone with whom I could make my own life, in a way separate from the past. Possibly, I knew Bernd would be very demanding. I have always been sad that Bernd and I could not stay in contact. My husband Henri and I and our children would have welcomed him at all times. I also understand how Bernd felt. He had no father, and had to take on many responsibilities. He thought that he was alone. He wasn't, but he had his choices, as I had mine, so we cannot regret. Bernd and I might have had an extraordinary life together – but I believe it could have been one destined to end badly. With Henri I have found something most women still have only an idea of. That is, a kind and loving man, a fulfilled life, fine children. I hope Bernd will read this and be glad for me.'

Minou was interested to hear of my week with Bernd, and interrogated me closely about his health and state of mind.

The latter, I elected to reassure her, was rather good. She laughed at that. 'You English – rather good – what a perfectly subtle phrase.' When we parted, her small, gloved hand still in mine, she said: 'I think it is too late and too difficult for anything storybook to occur for Bernd and I. Do please let me know if there is something I can do for him. Or, of course, if there is anything he wishes to say to me.' The comment was left in the air. I took the chance to say to her: 'I think it would only be that he loves you.' She smiled and responded: 'I know that, but it is nice to hear it said – even second-hand.'

The ensuing months were spent in the tedium of the proofs and the final legal permissions that are the precursors to print. My direct contacts with Bernd were infrequent and indirect, except for a couple of brief calls he made to me in the small hours and when he was drunk. Dwight acted as intermediary and kept me in touch with his friend's decline in health. Louis remained conscientious in his supervision of the Töst estate, despite his age and intrinsic reluctance for the role. That is to say, he guarded the papers, writings and film material and its copyright status. There was no known Will, since Töst had no property or indeed money. Dwight told me that there was a notarised letter in which Töst specified that ownership of all his work was in the hands of Dwight and Minou, who had absolute discretion over its disposal. This pleased Louis, who was keen to divest himself of his responsibilities. It seemed that Bernd was tidying up his life.

There was a long silence from Töst over the winter of 2002 – 3. Because of the impending publication it was essential to ensure that the legal protections against suit and on behalf of the estate were in place. There was also, with the papers he left with Dwight, a letter to Minou, and by inference, her children. The contents were barred from publication, although Dwight kindly sent me a copy. Suffice to say they very tenderly and movingly reciprocated the sentiments Minou had expressed in her one interview, though without regret or apology.

In the February of 2003, we – that is, Dwight – had a postcard with a 'Dear all' salutation, from Paradise Bend, Florida. It noted that Töst had found a 'crazy Yank antique dealer with whom I can finish my days drunk and possibly happy. Today we drink the wine; tomorrow we dig the gold'. That was it. On Thanksgiving Day of the same year, Dwight called me to say that Bernd had been found dead in a boat on Lake Okeechobee. The cause of death was unknown but foul play was not suspected. What emerged, of course, according to Dwight, was simply that Töst, already suffering from serious liver disease, had seemingly gone one bottle too far – quite likely, on purpose – and chosen this odd Floridian waterscape as the place to end his life.

Dwight had Bernd Töst's body shipped back to the USA for cremation on Staten Island. He sent the ashes to me in London and, through Louis Bates, I sent them on to Minou. A while later, she wrote a short letter from a hotel in Esbjerg. She had been to North Frisia and scattered Bernd among the sand dunes. So we sent this book to print at last.

Chapter Five
Epilogue

Just as the proofs of this book were ready to print, my publisher had for various reasons to reschedule his priorities. So, as sometimes happens, publication was deferred and we all got on with our normal lives. Then, in the Autumn of 2005, I received a small package. It had been sent from the Bahamas. Inside was an audio-tape. There was no covering note. I put the tape into my cassette player. There was the sound of liquid being poured, a throat being cleared and then a familiar voice saying, 'Hi Bruno, guess who?' It was hard to know how to react. I switched off the tape. Was he still alive after all? Was I to be glad if he were, or furious to have been conned, or dismayed at the prospect of a rewrite for the book? All three occurred simultaneously. Later, when the day had been done with, I settled in my study and, with a glass of Scotch to hand, switched on the tape again. Forgive me for sharing Bernd's final joke with you in this way – but his story has been told how he chose and this is part of it. Other than ironing out minor infelicities in his narrative – Bernd wasn't always sober when dictating – this is his story, in his words as always:

'You are probably pretty pissed at me, Bruno babes. I don't blame you, and I should probably have stayed dead. Well, as it happens, I may be dead by the time you get this, or the day after, or whenever. The docs tell me that my guardian angel's getting old and tired and has put me on probation, but as there's no more gold digging to be done I might as well drink the wine.

'Why, how, what and so forth, I hear you cry. You were

square with me, Bruno, and, as the book hasn't appeared so far as I know, I guess my curiosity and maybe vanity were piqued, teased or something. Most likely your publisher has got chicken over a book about a has-been porn filmmaker. In to-day's moral majority thing, it's unlikely to feature on the coffee tables of whomever the fuckwits are who set the so-called tone.

'Be that as it may, you can, if you wish, call Dwight and vent your wrath on him. To give him credit, he didn't like the idea, but went along with it from loyalty. I feel bad about Minou and have no idea what to do. Something will occur. It would be great though if you would send her a copy of the book, should it appear, or just final typescripts so she and my nephews have something to explain bad BB.

'So, as you know from my postcard, I'd met up with this insane but lovable Irish-American called Phil.

'I'd taken a train to New Orleans, and that's another story. Something to do with wondering why I was going back to LA and the train being such a peaceful, leisurely world where no one could reach me and there were no decisions to be made. Plus there were so many new places to see and I didn't want to just drift back ill and tired to the old life. Whatever, New Orleans sounded fun. So I was in this bar off Bourbon – where else? – and watching the local football team get hammered. Their reputation wasn't so hot so there was more derisory laughter than groans. Next to me was this big guy. Crumpled, but his clothes had cut, you know. We were obviously the outsiders and anyway, hard drinkers recognise each other so we began to talk, as you do. I've always liked the way men edge into conversation in these situations. It's clipped, monosyllabic. Not at all like women where it's all the news you need and more in ten seconds flat.

'Phil is – I should now say, was – an antique dealer. Originally he was a marine colonel and then a banker. Being an antique dealer was just something to do between drinks. We both laughed a lot about our respective professions, though we were interested too in each other's line of work. Anyway, despite his being a marine and all that, he was also the sort of alcoholic who has a problem with being out on his own. So when he fell off his stool and the motherly old soul behind the bar became hostile I had to get Phil out of there.

'He was generally an agreeable drunk, if slightly uncertain in temper. This time he was co-operative and I got him back to his boarding house at the top end of a street near the cemetery. His landlady was a Creole mama right out of central casting called Madame Leonora. I mention this trivial detail because she was a good person and if you go to New Orleans you should go see her and give her my thanks. Except she may be dead as she was damned ancient when I met her. Her first words were, "What you done to my Colonel Phil?" But she was used to him so we put him to bed and she asked me to supper, which was how I got a room there. Phil and I wandered around New Orleans for a week buying junk for his antique shop in Paradise Bend, Florida. After this he asks about my plans, which are zero, and he wonders if I'd care to drive back to Florida with him in his U-Haul as it's a long way and he could use the help. This is fine with me and we get on, so we set off. Some people may wonder if there is a gay agenda here. There isn't. Men can be real buddies without a homoerotic subtext or whatever the pointy-head liberal shits think. I have to tell you that two men in their sixties who have led less than healthy lives do not present well sexually, especially to each other. It's all piss and wind as they say, and as Phil remarked one morning in a motel we stopped at, having seen me go into the shower naked, "Your bare ass makes me glad I'm not gay."

'I told him I had no licence and insurance but he said it didn't matter and me driving let him drink. We had a pretty good trip all things considered and managed to cover a lot of ground in our experience and view of the world, without at this stage becoming too Oprah Winfrey. He'd known Madame Leonora since his time in Nam, when her son had been a master sergeant in his command and was killed in action, but had previously won some valour medal, like a silver star or oak-leaf cluster or whatever. He had visited her with her boy's things and they became good friends. The antiques business followed a high-level career with this fancy bank, which ended in early retirement and a divorce. That was his second wife. The first had dumped him when he was in Vietnam. He told me he had shelled out a huge settlement that mostly involved his New York apartment and pension. "Tough," he said to me as we drove through the Panhandle, "but that stinking bitch and her crap lawyer missed my real cash and my overseas property."

'By strange chance, we passed by de Funiak Springs. You remember it was where that girl in *Super Bitch* who liked it in the ass came from. As it was evening we checked into a Howard Johnson and went into town. It's a quite pretty, if sleepy place. There's an old railway train there and it used to be some kind of railhead. Phil wondered if the girl was still there and would she like to be fucked in the ass for old time's sake. I couldn't remember her name or what she looked like, but was glad to have seen her hometown. Pretty well all those good girls vanished back into the straight world. I often wonder if somewhere in their lingerie drawer isn't a photo book or spool or tape of them getting it on that would blow the kids' minds when they found it. Just imagine: "Oh look, what's this, holy cow, oh *no*, it's mom doing, *what?* Oh, *gross!*"

'Rolling down I-75 toward Paradise, Phil tells me the town is something of a state attraction. He hit on it when doing some training in the swamp stuff of which Florida has a good deal. There's no great reason for it, but somehow it just grew until half the town centre is junk – I should say antique and curio – shops. It is pretty well out of the way though. Everyone has a reason for sliding off the map. I didn't ask him about why. Let the other guy tell you what he wants to tell you.'

There is a long pause here, the chink of glass and the sound of liquid, some rustling. Faintly, a woman's voice says 'Hi honey, you OK?' and Bernd's response comes: 'Yeah, good.'

The tape is switched off.

'Good morning, Bruno, so sorry to cut you off last night. Had to take time out. You may wonder who the lady was. Well, that's no lady; that's my live-in housekeeper and good companion Lindy. I am very fortunate to have a personable young woman who in return for free board and lodging and a decent expense allowance will cook, wash and mend plus provide entertaining conversation and from time to time suck my cock whilst I fondle and reciprocally pleasure her sleek young body. She tolerates a fuck if my cock is working, but seems to prefer my tongue anyway for orgasmic pleasures. She has a lively sexual imagination of her own and we have explored some interesting territory in that context. Nor does she rebuke me for being a lush. In fact, she is every old man's dream. I have no idea why she picked me, but she did. We both have a safe haven, there are no strings, the relationship will terminate not too far hence and so we can just enjoy each other, which we do, very much.

'Yes, onto Paradise, so hopefully and romantically named. Phil and I arrived in torrential rain, it being late on in a bad hurricane season. Tourism is not much started, nothing opens before noon and everything shuts down by 5pm. If we do $200 a week in the summer we are doing well. Phil's shop is in an arcade and has a shared washroom with the café next door. He's kind of made his number there and although the owner is something of a grouch, the head girl is an all-American cutie who admires Phil's marine credentials. As do most of the town's jocks including the sheriff and the fire chief and his crew. So Phil is an honorary member of the buffalo rangers and the alligator army and whatever good ole boy, redneck groups have by way of socialising. It involves mostly shooting guns, drinking beer and having barbecues. This is fine by me. Phil has decided my actual career needs some editing for the locals. In a brilliant introduction at some event or other he manages to compress my exotic parentage – son of legionnaire father – with escape from occupied Europe and subsequent involvement with 'stuff' in New York and LA. The inferences are clear. After that, all I have to do is laugh in the right places and say "You bet," and I'm one of the team. In fact, the sheriff came up to me a few days later in the street and put his arm on my shoulder – he was all of 6 foot 6 and 300lb – and said, "Bernie, here in Paradise, what a man was is gone. What he is now, is what counts with us." I nearly broke up thinking about the theological undertones of this.

'Still, it was all very agreeable. Phil's house is a decent-sized, classic frame house from the 1930s or 1940s. It is on a generous lot in a long, quiet, tree-lined street only a gentle ten-minute walk from the shop. I have my own room and bathroom. My role is simply to do the food marketing, mind the shop when Phil is too bored, drunk or indeed absent, and give him a hot dinner a couple of times a week. This includes running barbecues when he invites his pals around which is about once a month. This may sound a tad subservient, if not cute, but truth is, I was broke, Dwight had done enough for me and it was perfectly pleasant work.

'As I said, mostly Phil was a cheerful drunk – and given I kept reasonable pace with him on the drinks, I could handle repetitive rambling without pain. Usually he then just flaked out and all I did was ensure he wasn't going to choke to death. On odd occasions he could get angry and abusive. Since this was never in public I just told him to go fuck himself and went to bed. In the morning we carried on as usual; no big deal. He was never sick – to my knowledge – or pissed or shitted himself, and never insulted a woman – at least, not intentionally. He was a real John Wayne kind of guy. Yeah.

'The hurricane, when it hit, was goddamn amazing. Black low sky like living under Satan's belly and rain that crashed down like the belly had been slit. Then the wind that tore nails from battens, locks from shutters and the roofs off all the poorer houses and left the trailer parks in a shambles. Phil and I were in the basement of his house with a bottle of Scotch for diversion as the storm executed its dance. The lights went out. We cursed the loss of power since we had some dish or other in the oven. Far off we heard the fire-engine sirens. Phil wondered if we should call the sheriff and offer our services. Luckily, the phones were down too and Phil had lost his cellphone. So we stayed put and ate potato chips and wondered if the new waitress in the Paradise Grill gave head. We were just old men in a small town with some drama outside and lewd thoughts inside. We lost a couple of roof tiles, the attic window shutter blew off and there was a leak in the dormer of Phil's room. That said, Louise or Denis or whomever the hurricane was named after passed on and we were fine. Even if some swathes of Paradise – sadly but as usual the less privileged – were fucked.

'Speaking of which, Phil and I found it possible to discuss being fucked. In business terms we had a surprising amount in common. Whatever business you are in there are always the people with the money, power or influence. If you are one of them you can fuck anyone. If you are not one of them, you need to be in their frame of reference as useful or interesting, or you're fucked. Well, I should add that if you are in their frame you are fucked anyway. This is no different from the mediaeval court. You pitch up, make your play and if it works you have a game on. Jesus Christ, Bruno, you should know that too. Then there's being fucked in the sex sense. Phil got mighty interested in the fact I had been a sex filmmaker. If only because he assumed I had fucked hundreds of women. I told him, no, I haven't, although I have watched hundreds of women being fucked. I pointed out he had been married twice, which is also a highly informative experience. For myself, however many women I had fucked, there was never a commitment, only a temporary engagement. You'll be thinking, Bruno, my friend, about Minou. Ah yes, but not in this context.

'As you know, Bruno, I like women a lot as fellow human beings, though they can be a pain in the ass at times. I reckon they have had a tough deal in many respects. Still, I am a man and I can't think like a woman. All I know is, most women like sex, or wish they liked it better, and if they are hetero, they really like men and cocks. So a good fuck is something we all like but evidently women are more picky and it's obvious why.

Thus men have to have a discourse about women and fucking. I mean, we like fucking women and we can find out they like fucking us. But it's hard to get up close and personal unless you are real buddies or total strangers and, of course, drunk. You'll notice, Bruno, old friend, and I am slightly miffed you didn't make more of it in our book, that in my movies, it's mostly hard to tell who is fucking whom – *capisce?*

'Be that as it may, Phil had a huge TV and a satellite and this gizmo that gave you twenty four programmes on-screen at once, which he would watch, scanning over what's on and giving maybe a few minutes of attention to the full screen version. I mean we watched *War and Peace* for five minutes, but missed the war bit. Phil says, "Phooey, that guy Tretchikov just wants to screw the bimbo in the big dress. He should say so." His menu has, of course, got loads of adult channels from everywhere. These, he spends time with – ball games and financial news the only others to rate attention – especially when he's truly out of it. His pretext is that I'm a professional and must be interested and can tell him what's so sexy about the action.

'Mostly the answer is nothing in any rational sense, but if the chicks are pretty and the guys aren't like Quasimodo, the old mouth, cock, cunt and ass combo still has the key ingredients. So we sit, we two old men sliding into oblivion, and watch these hard-working kids locked together and he goes, "Wheeoo, do they really go for that?" or, "Jeez, that guy has some cannon. What do you think Bernie?" And I'm thinking, at least these kids aren't holding up gas stations or stealing cars. Or, they look or don't look like they are having fun, or, she's like someone I knew, or, the lighting is crap, or, isn't digital great, I wish I'd had it and so forth. But none of this is of interest to Phil, except marginally, so I mostly go,

"Yeah Phil, this is a good one" or, "Frankly, Phil, this stinks." If the second, he grunts "You're the professional, Bernie" and switches to the news or the ball game. I tried to get him to watch *Apocalypse Now* one night on the basis that he was the professional in relation to this one. He wouldn't do it. "Fuck you, Bernie, you weren't there, you have no idea. Watch it all you want, I'm going to bed."

'I was interested in the issue of attractive men versus dorks. Not liking men sexually, I get puzzled as to why really class women go for gross guys. I mean, I can see how some young guy with a great body and a shapely cock is attractive, but there are some hairy-assed, scrawny scrotum sleazes out there. This isn't to do with the mystery of love, it's just about visual sex. I think I was a tad naïve sometimes and tried too hard. The jerk-off audience is quite happy to see itself balling a nice chick, or even some old turkey like their wife, I expect. This is a poor line of enquiry. Sex is in the head. I was wondering if the fact that Phil and I had some interest in the size and aesthetics of other men's cocks made us closet fags. I don't think so. Part of the reason his wives divorced him was his incessant hunt for blow jobs. My films are my thesis. You'll note there is a lot of fucking in my movies, whereas the lingua franca – to coin a phrase – of male sex fantasy is mostly about oral sex, and increasingly, anal sex. The good old Marquis had a lot to say about that. He felt women were more pleasured and less at risk from oral or anal sex and that the men certainly got off on it better. This is not what I have heard about anal from most women, though girls are usually very comfortable with cocksucking and very switched on by guys who give head. I think, Bruno, this is enough for tonight. I've gotten introspective and rambling and Lindy is out and it's my turn to put something in the pan for dinner. Oysters, perhaps, I feel horny thinking about sex. Bruno, this little machine and you are turning into my confessional. Oysters? I wish. There in Paradise Bend it was steak and fries, here it's conch scallops.

'Hi, time has passed as it does and the theme is my life with Phil. His agenda for me became increasingly clear when he fell into one of his drunken rages and accused me of sponging off him. I told him it was jake with me if I left that night and he said "Don't be stupid, who's going to mind my store?" He had a boat down on Lake Okeechobee that he liked to hang out on and, when possible, have someone take him out fishing, since he was usually too drunk to navigate safely. The fact was that I had been looking after his store since we met. He would let me open up, come in for about an hour around noon and then shuffle off to meet his pals somewhere. To be fair, he was, even when drunk, not too obviously so: just very loquacious, witty and affable. He was generous with it, and gave out presents all the time from his stock, especially to ladies. There was a regular stream of gaudily-dressed and over-made-up matrons driving in from Miami and the Gulf Coast to flirt with Phil and, whether they spent any money or not, they'd always leave with some gewgaw.

'It became then a routine that every so often I would drive Phil down to Clewiston where his boat was, and hand him over to the good folk at the bar by the marina who knew and tolerated, if not loved him. Then I'd drive all the way back to the Bend and mind the store until Phil or someone rang to tell me he was ready to come home. Which sometimes meant right now and mega-fast, because he has gotten to be truly out of it. There was a woman who ran a bed and breakfast place there who had a soft spot for Phil and who, I suspect, gave him more bed than breakfast. She was handsome enough in a beaten-up way. There are loads like her in America, running bars and serving in cheap restaurants: tough, fast-talking, possibly once tender women who have had a less than square deal. On one occasion, Phil said, after we had gone a mile or so from town, "That Irene has her eyes on me. Do you think I should marry her?" How the fuck would I know? Sure, Phil, third time lucky. You're rich, she's poor and you're both beat-up oldsters. Sounds perfect. He called me a cold-hearted son of an army mule and went to sleep. We got stopped once by a state trooper ten miles out of Clewiston; no reason, just routine curiosity and something about illegal hunters. Not having a licence had me mumbling but Phil suddenly woke up, produced his own licence and some military ID and barked "OK trooper, this man is my driver." The poor guy backed up and saluted and said "Yessir, thank you, Colonel" and Phil went, "Well done, Officer, well done." I loved him for that. It was the sheer tone of command and the switch from the trooper put-down to the officer respect bit that impressed me. There is this ruling class thing I learned first in England and could never quite handle.

'You probably wonder why these tapes came from the Bahamas, and whether I'm still here, and how come. It's a fair question. Phil had a house here on one of the smaller island cays. Not grand, but comfortable and beachside on the lagoon – and he had a dock as well for his boat. Nothing fancy, like the one on Okeechobee; just a 32-foot powerboat with a couple of bunks, a head, swim platform and a flybridge. The sort of thing you could shoot over to the next island in for lunch. We went there a couple of times at the back end of '02 and into the Spring of '03, mostly for the fishing. I am truly sorry about the dropout and deception thing, but I just wanted to get out of everything. Dwight has been a real friend so don't blame him for it. After all, nothing got screwed up. He'll pass on anything you want to send me. I really love these islands. No tax and Brit legal tradition, hence a more manageable bureaucracy, but near the USA for the basic essentials. Enough of the plug; here was where I met Lindy. There's not that many bars and so forth and people kind of go to them in turn depending on which have the happy hour or the dinner special that night but as everyone knows each other and wants to share the business, it gets regularised. Friday is the Tikki Bar and by the time we get there on this particular trip Phil is fairly lit up. But he's being funny and Lindy is our "wait-person" as we now must say. She has a very neat butt and great legs and there is a lot to be seen of them. Also she has fantastic eyes and a special smile. So I am suddenly and, for the first time for decades, in love. There are a couple of acquaintances from the yacht club with us and the badinage is flowing and Lindy looks after us. Is it my imagination, or does she sparkle a little more for me?

'How, indeed why, can I share this with you? I think because I can't make films any more and this narrative makes it real. So what happened? Phil reaches terminal condition and announces himself bored and the yacht club group has gone. I ask for the tab. Lindy goes, "Oh, this early, I was enjoying you guys." I tell her I have to see my pal home. She says, "Why don't you come back later?" I can feel the kick in my belly and, you know, I almost cry with pleasure. Phil goes home quietly and lies, or indeed falls, down in front of the TV. I leave the car and get out the bike – nowhere is far away. In the Tikki Bar it is nearly closing time. Lindy appears, taking off her apron, and says, "I thought you'd never come." We have a drink at the bar and exchange credentials. Lindy is mixed Yank and Aussie. She's an English literature major from somewhere and wants to be a journalist. She's twenty-four and was married for six months to a violent rancher in Queensland. Being in the Bahamas was a whim as she retreated from Australia. I tell her I am seventy and a sometime pornographic filmmaker acting as butler to a Yankee alcoholic. I have never been married but I spent several terrific years with my kid sister. Lindy's eyes go wide and her beautiful lips are parted. She leans into me and her hand rests on my knee. "Bernie," she says, "that's the most exciting biography I've ever heard." We have another drink and talk some more about life, the world and stuff; you know. Including our star signs, which we don't, of course, believe in. I think we both know that we have crossed some watershed and that what we are doing now is filling in time before we make decisions.

'The barman tells us it's last-drink time and Lindy says, "Bernie, do you like oral sex – I mean, doing it to a woman?" I say I do, very much. She says, "I've never had it, and I want it and you seem a good sort of person to do it for me." At times like this you get sad the world is often so unkind to pretty girls, and glad too that room has been left for you to provide comfort. Her place is just a couple of rooms and a bathroom at the back of the docks. Inside, she turns and says, "Can I trust you?" To which the only answer is, if you don't think you can, babes, say goodnight now. Listen, I tell her, let's make it easy, just like on the movies. You're feeling horny, you want your pussy sucked and you have a guy who is waiting on the bed for you to come and sit on his face – or however you like it.

'She laughs at this. "Yes, on your face, Bernie. Just let me go and freshen up, as they say.' Your call, I reply. The thing is, Bruno, I need to go through this because it's a spectacular memory to have. That Lindy and I are still together and having fun is a bonus, but this was like losing my virginity again. I remove my shirt because there is nothing like a girl's thighs against your body, but leave my pants on so as not to presume, if you know what I mean. Then she comes back in and is naked below the waist. I think how subtle that cue is. Her cunt needs attention, but her tits are still private. Later, she said my keeping my pants on had really convinced her. There is not much artifice required. She straddles me amidships and lets me take her in, feel the silk and muscle of her thighs. Then she moves forward and over so her belly and bush are centre-frame. I have my palms cupping her buttocks and feel her pause for a moment. Then she's down onto my face, her fingers in her groin, parting the fur and the lips. There's a smell of soap and something much better. She sighs, I take a breath, some preparatory sniffs and tongue flicks and we're feeding each other. She has gone to the magic kingdom while I am in the best restaurant in the world. It's kind of fade to black at that moment because that close, the detail gets lost. Still it was just huge pleasure and when she came I think I must have come with her, at least psychologically.

'She rested for a while, sprawled out, so I could admire her general torso. Then she looked across to me and kissed me before noticing there was blood on my lips. The pubic bone is tough on lips. After that we were pals. I'd see her most days in the bar, though we didn't have sex again. She was very warm, even affectionate, but nothing was said. Lindy had all the communication things and Phil had net access, so we promised to keep in touch when I went back to Florida. In fact, I found myself sitting at Phil's laptop doing little chatty notes to this girl and having her reply, just like real people. Is this love? In a way, of course, it is. But it isn't the thing you know will carry you forever. It's just something about a nice recollection with no regrets or recriminations. At least, that's the way she and I have spelled it out. That said, she had – I should say has – some of the insouciance of Minou, the motherliness of Noreen and the sexual heat of Sonja. Which, even diluted, is powerful juju for me.

'Lindy was pretty keen to come back to the States with us. I mentioned this to Phil, who looked hard at me with his marine colonel look. "You're balling this female and you want her under my roof, you chicken-shit, polack creep?" I pointed out that I wasn't a polack and anyway Lindy could keep house for us. "You keep house," Phil retorted. "I don't want more mouths to feed." I suggested Lindy might fuck us both in due course. This was pretty mendacious of me, but you know, what do you expect? Phil sneered. "If I wanted real sex I wouldn't watch those God-awful movies you're so proud of making." I mention all this only to show how desperate I was to have Lindy around. I figured if I got her over there, everything would work out. You may wonder why I suddenly had this desire for regular female company. Well, Lindy was just perfect. We had fun conversations, she emailed me that she had totally decided being sucked off was her big thing, and that fooling around with my dick would be fine too. At seventy these are opportunities not to be missed. What's more, I started to feel better. I drank less – tough to do in Phil's company – began to ride the bike more and so on.

'Having mentioned that Phil was not keen on her joining us and had suggested she would be acceptable only if she had sex with him – sorry guys – Lindy just shrugged it off. "So, I have money, I'll rent somewhere nearby and get a job in one of those antique places or wherever and we can carry on as normal." Phil and I went back to Florida and Lindy came to the Bend a month or so later. Because of what I'd said, she was pretty frosty with Phil at first. In due course I straightened it out, but it was a close call in our relationship.

'As it happened, Phil took to Lindy. He helped her get a job with his local attorney and was always charming to her. This may have been in part because he had himself hooked up with a stylish divorcee from Sarasota via Philadelphia, whom he met in the shop on one of the days he had appeared. She was a nice-looking, crisply dressed and intelligent woman, but had decided she would not take things further than social unless Phil gave up drinking. This led to some truly shitty days when we would drive Phil to Sarasota or Boca Grande, or wherever the rendezvous was for lunch or dinner – believe me, we're talking hundreds of fucking miles. We'd sit around talking polite crap the way they do in middle America, or middle anywhere come to that, completely fucking sober. Moderately oiled, Phil was outstanding company. Dull as a drain sober. Lindy and I, positioned by Phil as business partner and fiancée, struggled along, at times comatose, at others barely able to stop laughing. The only benefit was that we'd get back to Phil's, and we'd all get drunk. Phil would go to sleep and Lindy and I would just lick and snuffle at each other in my room or at her place until we had had enough.

'The lady, Marsha, I think, disappeared over the horizon. We reverted to the routine. Except I missed a few of the good ole boy sessions due to Lindy, who suddenly announced she needed a break and was off to LA for a few days, or weeks possibly.

'Well, nothing is forever, so I said of course, whatever, and come back soon y'all. She and I had a very nice evening before I drove her to the airport in Phil's spavined Chevy. As we kissed in that light way only habituated or possibly about to part forever couples have, she said, "Did you know Phil has made you sole executor and beneficiary of his Will?" I expressed surprise. She said, "He is a very ill and very rich man." I sighed and told her to get the hell out of the car and see you when I see you, sweet-lips, but take care. Her response was to say, "You're the one with the sweet lips," and squeeze my crotch.

'Somehow that bit of information about Phil made me sure she'd be back – more than the crotch squeeze. It was a good thought, even if it had somewhat disquieting undertones.

'Phil was drinking harder than ever. He rarely came to the shop and I found I was enjoying the business and cooking and generally feeling useful. I could still kill a bottle of scotch with Phil in the evening but as he'd already done at least one by noon this put him ahead by a margin. As I said, I was feeling better and began to wonder whether death was back in his office pulling out someone else's file. Phil and I got along fine – he'd get peevish sometimes and accuse me of neglect, so I'd close the shop and go cook him a meal and hang one on with him. His friend the fire chief came in one day and, after enquiring about Lindy – whom the boys had taken to, unsurprisingly, and by the way whose evident relationship with me gave me terrific credentials – said he was kind of worried about "the Colonel". I put my concerned face on and shared the issue. In truth I had no idea what to do. It was his life. All I could manage was to keep him fed, and look after his business; be a pal. Tell me, Al, what do you think? We shook our heads in manly sorrow and then shook hands in equally manly solidarity.

'Two or three weeks after Lindy had gone, Phil decided it was time to go to the boat on Okeechobee. It was pretty close to Thanksgiving. I drove him down and we stopped in the liquor store in Clewiston and stocked him with scotch – he loved scotch and often apologised for not drinking bourbon or Irish whiskey. "It is my one disloyal act," he once said, "but at least scotch isn't made by the English." I remember saying, "Party time, Phil?" and he used his favourite phrase: "Today we drink the wine, tomorrow we dig the gold." Looking back, I was wondering why no beer, but nothing clicked.

'I stayed overnight on the boat with him – he had by this time become estranged from his ex-landlady. We drank too much scotch as usual and I drove back to the Bend damn carefully with a bad hangover. Though this was a good sign as Lindy pointed out. She was back, and sitting on Phil's porch in his swing chair looking pretty as a picture. Bruno, you are still quite a young man but possibly old enough to appreciate what it is like at age seventy to have a sexy girl embrace you, hug you, lead you off to the bathroom and fill a bath for you. And then to soap you down and tell you you were missed as she fondles your balls and rebukes you for your misdeeds. I didn't care then, still don't, what her designs are. I've come toward the end, and she has it all to do. Live the dream. I didn't ask what she was doing in LA and she didn't tell me. Instead we had a terrific afternoon in bed, as you can only do in the aftermath of a hangover. I knew this guy who had the theory that the reason men woke up in the morning after a heavy night, with a hard-on, was that their body thought it was going to die and needed to reproduce. That strikes me as credible. Anyway, we had some lunch and a bottle of wine and Lindy says she feels sexy, having missed me and now fooled around in the bath. To be fair to myself, I don't have a bad body for my age. It's still pretty smooth and there's no great belly and so forth. (Sorry, Bruno, you are getting what is going through my head; my body is of no interest to you.) I am very relaxed and have that sexual need that makes you look at a woman in a certain way and they know it, and if they want it too the frontiers are open.

'Moving swiftly on, we have just enjoyed a great fuck. She's not big on fucking, as I've said, but thinks she should get to like it as part of her healing process, she says. But this was good and my dick had done its stuff, which isn't guaranteed. Maybe it is my healthier regime, or maybe it is the attitude where I just wanted to fuck this bitch who'd left to go screwing around somewhere else and was anyway just setting me up for the usual old guy – young girl rip-off. Anyway, we called time from the fuck and after lying around panting and sweating, she'd taken it into her mind to go sixty-nine and suck my dick in a desultory if affectionate way. She said she liked her own taste. We lay on our sides and it was very pleasant to have my cock in her mouth and my head on her thigh while I looked up into her groin and admired the scenery once more. In due course I begin to lick around and she gets interested and is over me on her knees and we are going at it. I notice how pink and tight and sweet her asshole is and decide to kiss it. She likes that – a little gasp – but when my lips close on her she pushes back into me, so I stick my tongue into her and she squeaks and her hand tightens on my cock. Another idea occurs – for God's sake, I'm a porn film director – so I wet my fingers in her pussy and press into her asshole. More "mmm"s and her teeth are clenched onto my cock and my finger slides into her ass. I fuck her with it and she is humming away with my cock pressed to her cheek so I put another finger in and she begins to chew seriously on my dick and her hand reaches back under her belly and she begins to frig herself. We go on like this in an increasingly grunt and mmm and hunnnh way, with me finger-fucking her asshole, and gorging on mouthfuls of her cunt. While she jerks off, her knuckles pummelling my nose, we compete for her clit and she tries to suck and pull my cock from its moorings. We come pretty much within seconds of each other. Me by a short head, ho ho, which is great because cum is part of her scene and so she's next; and I think I could be killed, rupture her with my fingers in her ass, or both, she threshes and screams so much. I had never heard her like that until that time.

'This may be an embarrassment to you, Bruno, but trust me, it is central to this narrative. Unless you understand the sex bit you won't finish the story. Something big happened that afternoon. Maybe it was my giving her a straight arm fuck, or opening her ass, or what she had been doing in LA. Whichever is the case, she became softer, more dulcet in her voice and looks. Just like that. When we sat down to supper that evening we were truly like a couple. I had stopped being seventy and she had stopped being a slightly phony tough, victim chick. We had got it together.

'Over the next couple of days, I mind the shop and Lindy wanders round town and reconnects the way girls do. She reports that general opinion is it's good she's back and the fact she's shacked up with me while Colonel Phil is away is OK too. Some of the churchier group disapproves as always, but the Colonel's military history, the fact we behave like gentlefolk in public and Lindy's personal charm makes it fine with the main social authorities. Then late one afternoon, as Lindy and I are just back home and thinking about supper, we get the phone call. It's the sheriff in Clewiston. Phil has been found dead on his boat and could we tell his attorney and as I am his partner, get on down for some formalities.

'Lindy and I spent a thoughtful evening. It would be a lie to say I was grief-stricken, but he had been a good friend at a time when I needed one. We'd had some laughs, got to know each other and shared as much in a short time as many men share in a life. Lindy had less of a regret problem, though I could tell she sympathised – or, Bruno, is it empathised nowadays? – with my tristesse. That said, I think there were some dollar signs floating over her head as she casually remarked, "Oh, darling, I wonder how much he's worth." I had been honey and sweetie, but this was the first time for darling.

'Since Phil had long since given me signature access to his checking account, which never had less than $250,000 in it, I was able to make her lips part with anticipation as she took that on board and added up the property and fantasised about secret offshore funds. There is something weirdly erotic about watching an attractive woman getting to grips with your net worth as opposed to any other attribute you may have. Given a satisfactory evaluation, you can see this is very akin to having an orgasm, probably better – there is a great song about that involving diamonds. I always liked Monroe's version best. Truism it may be, but seeing it in action is fabulous. If I were in the movie business I think I'd make a film called *Dick and His Money Go Hunting*. Just kidding, they are mostly like that. Except the ones called *Nancy and Her Purse Go Hunting*. Go on, remind yourself of some of them.

'We got up early after a cuddlesome but comfortably sexless night and reached Clewiston by 10.00hrs., as Phil liked to describe time. His attorney arrived shortly after. I knew the sheriff a little so we exchanged the usual crap and drove over to the morgue and there was Phil on the tray, deadly pale and deadly dead. I missed his light-blue eyes and the way they pinned me down when I disagreed and he said, "Just fucking do it, Bernie," and I missed his arm raised as he bellowed, "Drink flowing like glue here." The county coroner would have to do his thing but the police doctor and we all agreed on the cause. We signed stuff that would have the body shipped to the Bend for cremation and a service since that was where his friends were. The attorney, Lindy and I went to a bar and had coffee. He told Lindy she could have her job back, but she smiled kindly and said no, thanks all the same. That out of the way he confirmed that as I was in charge of the business and cash already it would be fine to carry on, and that I was the sole beneficiary. In due course titles, deeds and other material documentation would be available and he'd be real glad to act for me. Why not, who else? So we shook hands and everyone was totally happy. The attorney had a client, I was rich and Lindy had an old fool she could wrap around... well, I thought about that and became dizzy.

'I let Lindy drive us back to Paradise Bend, to give me time to think. In any case, I like watching women drive. They sit differently and their posture is alert in a certain way and their thighs are unselfconsciously apart. When they drive they exercise their own competence, and anyone doing something individual that they concentrate on and do well is interesting and attractive to watch. The main result of my thought is evident. Provided Dwight would do this, I could fake my own demise and, I am sorry to say, pull the shutters on the rest of the world. No, I'm not sorry. This is my life. There was that past bit that is public and the now which is mine. The sheriff of Paradise Bend had it right. Then Lindy: I wasn't prepared to make big plans, or to live with the suspicions of her managing me into an early reunion with Phil. That may seem unworthy, but Christ, Bruno, these girls are deep-down devious survivors. She played some country station on the radio and occasionally patted my knee and said "OK, sweetie?" It was very soothing stuff because I knew there were no more demands, issues or problems: just me and life and death. Wonderful, isn't it, what a little money can do. Forget the reputation thing, net worth only comes with a dollar sign in front of it.

'A week on, and the undertakers have the body and the funeral is set. I don't think Phil has a church but something tells me Episcopalian will suit his inner and iconoclastic temperament. It appealed more to me anyway. The minister is well disposed, the good 'ole boys are heartwarmingly supportive and Paradise Bend gets set for a fine funeral for a true American hero. Lindy, of course, takes a leading role. Demurely dressed – for once foregoing her butt-enhancing designer shorts – she manages caterers and florists. All I have to do is think about some kind of address.

'The funeral is, in fact, fantastic. It is a warm but breezy day and the flags are out and the cortège proceeds with dignity from the house to the church. The coffin is, of course, draped with the Stars and Stripes, as befits a national hero, but I had reminded the fire chief that Phil had Confederate leanings and there was a judicious sprinkling of stars and bars from some home flagpoles en route. All the sermons and addresses are on the same theme – that of the great American – and why not? Phil was certainly as good an American as anyone around. By the time we have heard these stirring speeches and sung a few heartwarming hymns I am getting pretty emotional. Lindy is beside me in a formal but utterly becoming costume and a wide-brimmed black hat. She should be my daughter and I am momentarily overcome with a love of almost entirely non-sexual nature.

'It is my turn to speak. Haltingly I tell people that, as a humble immigrant to the United States of America from a war-torn Europe, I have nothing but respect for their great country. I have been honoured to work with and be the friend of, yes, a great gentleman and American. I hope to remain with my lovely fiancée – herself of American parentage on her father's side – as good and useful members of the Paradise Bend community that I have come to love so well. This goes down fine – maybe because I sort of mean it – and I feel the susurration of approval, even from the hatchet-faced Presbyterian dowagers who have appeared despite their reservations.

'I can't tell you how great the wake was back at Phil's place. Lindy had excelled herself, as had the caterers. I doubt the town had eaten and drunk so well since G.W. Armitage endowed and opened the new high school. They certainly all seemed to be there. Except, of course, the trailer trash, whose curious scouts were seen off by the sheriff's finest, themselves equal recipients of our hospitality. So by the time people bailed out and the caterers had gone and we were alone it was getting dark. I sat on the porch and watched lights come on and the town become still. Lindy is standing in front of me and I say how much I appreciate her support. Then I look up and see she is stark naked. "Come on, Bernie," she says. "I'm very very horny and I need you a lot."

'What with everything I am feeling pretty fucking good myself. The old dong gets itself up in sensible time, not least because Lindy is being particularly erotic, but maybe too because I am in good mental and physical form. We fool around doing the usual nice things and then she says, "Fuck my ass, Bernie, not with your fingers, with your cock." Then she rolls onto her belly and lifts her butt in an inviting way. There is nothing like a pretty woman with her haunches in the air. I can feel my gut going, "Yes, oh yes." I tell her, stay there I'll be back. Then I'm back with some Pond's Cream found in the bathroom and she's on her elbows and knees and has spread her legs to make things available. The bit of me that warns, "You're seventy and have erectile problems through fear and drink," is obliterated by the bit that says, "You have been asked to fuck a beautiful young woman who truly wants what you have to offer," though another bit helpfully adds, sotto voce, "and, by the way, she's still a bitch who wants your money."

'So I am hard as a bar and and her fingers clear the fur and stretch the lips just to make sure I have an unobstructed front-row view of the stage. I go down and give her the essential and in every way pleasant introduction of my tongue. Then I put the cold cream on my fingers and she squeaks at the coolness and sighs as her asshole opens easily and they slide in. After which I just get in position and look down on that most perfect sight and tease her by shoving into her cunt just for the feel, and then out and replace my fingers with my cock. She wants this and so, apart from a small gasp, works with me; relaxes and pushes back. Her asshole sucks my cock in. I hold her flanks and just go forward. It is tight and smooth and hot; and between us we work my cock into her until my balls are banging on her cunt and I can feel something soft high up in there against my dick head. Who cares. She is breathing harshly and then she groans and her hand comes back and feels my balls, and she collapses onto her belly under me and her buttocks sort of close and her rectum grips tight as a vice. I haven't got much to do. I can feel her fingers working away at her groin and she is squirming and heaving rhythmically and sort of panting and grunting stuff like oh and ah and fuck, Bernie, fuck. My dick is locked solid but her movement is working the skin around the muscle nicely; her sphincter is pulsing as if she's about to crap, which she said later she thought might happen too. But the whole thing is too well looked after and feels too sexy to care about things like that. I keep my weight balanced and divide my time between my own enjoyment and admiring her back and the way her face turned sideways on the pillow reflects her sexual sensations. It's all great. Her buttocks shove up into my belly and it is evident the boiler is going to blow. I tighten my grip on her hips and reciprocate. Thank God we have no close neighbours. At least one of us, if not both, is making sounds that replicate the moment of birth.

'Later on, we have recovered and done what's necessary and are lying side by side with a bottle of cold wine between us. She is purring at me and saying tender things. We schmooze each other for a while and then she tells me why she is not so hot on straight sex and is interested in up the ass – which she liked – or oral and its variations. She'd hinted previously about some hang-ups but now I got the full story. It turns out her crap husband pretty much raped her on their wedding night and after she had refused any more sex did some stuff that left her cunt somewhat damaged and her mental attitude even more so. This is more than you, or I, want to know really. I tell her that whatever she wants to enjoy is fine, but if she wants it in the ass on a regular basis, good practice says there are some sensible things to do and spontaneity is not an option. I hate being a pompous creep but I know this stuff professionally, and it has to be dealt with. Lindy doesn't too much like that line so leaning into my ear she whispers what she thinks would be nice as her best scenario. I'm always amazed how girlish even tough women can be. Why whisper?

'You might as well know, and then it's done with. I think it was terrific she could tell me. I guessed that her visit to LA was something to do with her sexual history. It would have made a great film, and I mean that seriously. What she really got off on was me with my fingers knuckle-deep inside her pussy, and my thumb and tongue working her clit, while she had a vibrator in her ass and sucked my dick. Now this didn't emerge as a prescription. It came out of a long conversation about what she enjoyed and didn't enjoy. It worked fine for me, and it worked very well for her. Why it worked for her is her affair, though it's hardly unfathomable. Why it worked for me was partly to do with my own sexual aesthetics, and partly because it worked filmically. I knew it would look exciting on screen. That said, we still get carried away and forget procedures and she is getting to like a straight fuck better.

'You don't often get to know how someone operates sexually in the detail we got to. Sensitive people can infer. Mostly I think men and women live and die in considerable ignorance of what the other gender's experience really is. That is, beyond basic metrics. How was it for you, however sincere a question, should not need to be asked. Don't you know, can't you tell? Given that we flatter to deceive, "why?" would be the better follow-up. It does occur to me that men would better understand women's experience of sex if they sucked cock or took it up the ass, at least now and again. I wonder if any wives use dildos on their menfolk. I never saw it in my time in Hollywood. I did see it done to a rent boy and on another occasion some woman wanted her husband buggered by a dominatrix. In fact, he wanted it and she was so out of her mind she thought it would be fun to watch. There were always some women scenes, of course. That seems another omission in my attempts to make films about sex. Now I have some money, maybe I can go back to work: just a thought.

'We settled down very nicely together in Phil's house. I had to buy Lindy a ring to back up the fiancée line, which led to another free and frank discussion between us that took me some time to think through. I told her that marriage was just not what I had in mind. On the other hand she was a great girl to have around and shouldn't feel I wasn't glad of her. I went to the attorney and had him transfer ownership of the antique business and the house to Lindy. The Bahamas and most of Phil's cash stayed with me and I made some kind of Will for it to go to Dwight when I died. By the way, Bruno, any money from the book if it ever gets published goes to you and I have assigned you all rights. Lindy had a little cry and said I was too generous, but she would have married me gladly if I asked. There it goes again. The syntax interested me. The use of "would have" to imply, "but the house etc., is good enough". End of problem. Except there is the "if I asked"; notice not "had" asked. This implies asking as still an option. If she'd been a bitch she'd have done something to try for the whole enchilada – or even get pregnant – but no, she's nice so she settles with a smile for about half a million bucks, but leaves the contract open for review! In fact, she told me she could find it difficult to get pregnant due to something that shitty ex of hers did to her. This is sad, if true, because she'd be a good wife and mother in my view. But this pregnancy stuff is like a secret weapon. Nonetheless she's had a tough break and as she is also somewhat in the role of daughter for me I want to give her a chance. That does not include becoming a father, however.

'It was a good thing I had done all this stuff because about six months later, Phil's second ex-wife apparently – I say this advisedly – pitches up with a claim she'd been bilked of a proper share in his estate. My attorney says that she really doesn't have a claim as the settlement included a full and final clause. However, as there is some faint prospect of a concealment and deception allegation, we might want to settle out of court to avoid a long and expensive action during which my assets are going to be frozen. So instead my ass is to be fried, I quip. To be honest, I think this has been set up by my attorney. I ask him what the buy-off will cost me. He sucks his teeth and says he will put an ex-gratia payment offer to the bitch, without prejudice nem fucking con and sub fucking judice. The lawyers settle at $50,000, which is a very suspicious sum. Why would this tramp settle for fifty grand when she is already rich and could possibly get ten times that? My attorney's fee is another ten thou on top of what he's already had from all the other stuff. I tell Lindy I've had it with the USA's rapacious legal system and will leave town before I'm stripped naked. I get my assets shipped over to the Bahamas to join what's already there and make the moves for permanent residency.

'"What do you want me to do?" asks Lindy. I tell her she has to decide that. As in, I know she wants me to say I want her to come to the Bahamas with me. We play these ridiculous mind-games for a while. I'll come if you want, do you want, you decide and so forth. Christ, women really do get convoluted. Take the risk, babe, tell me you want to come, and see if I say fuck off or great. Anyway, I'm too old to do this so I say if you want to come too that would be terrific, but if you don't I fully respect your need to pursue your life goals as you think best or some such bullshit. Then she goes, "What should I do with the house and the business?" I have possibly had too much scotch so I'm somewhat brusque. How the fuck would I know, it's your business and your house. Sell, rent or fucking set fire to it, honey; I'm not your goddamn father. Tears, sobs, rebukes like "no, but I thought you were my friend". She's right, I have been mean. I dry her tears and say I am a sour old fool and I love her, and her in the Bahamas would be not just great, but the best thing ever. So far as the property is concerned she could rent the house and lease the business or put a manager in. Either way she's got the worry over tenants and being ripped off. Then again the business is worth zip and the shop is effectively a rental, whereas the house is a tangible asset with a known value and possible growth potential. I am running out of sensible blah at this point and she is losing interest. Having recovered her poise she decides to get my cock out and make friends properly.

'One week later, she marches in waving some legal-looking papers and announces that she's got rid of the shop and the stock in a surprisingly good deal with the business next door who were dying to expand and are serious players. The house has been bought fully-furnished by our attorney who has always wanted it – and, I think, will make a few bucks from it too. However the price is a decent market valuation so why complain. The town is politely sorry we are leaving, but this is America so it happens. I give the car to the fire chief for his kids and we leave in a U-Haul en route to Miami to ship some pieces we thought Phil valued, and get ourselves over to Marsh Harbour. As we head east, with Lindy driving, I am thinking this is the first time I have felt financially and personally secure in my entire life. It's not altogether comfortable, but I'm kind of tired. Also the chick with the great legs and tits and determined jaw as she trundles our truck into the future makes it feel better. I lay down in the cab and put my head in her lap and went to sleep for a while.'

Bernd never bothered to put datelines on this series of recordings, so I can only guess at what time elapsed between any of the segments. This last seemed to show him in as mellow and contented a mood as at any time in our acquaintance.

'Well, Bruno, old boy, old pal, here in one of your jolly old British ex-colonies, now its own outstanding commonwealth of delectable islands, it is after 1800hrs and absolutely time for a peg or six. I am sitting on my lanai, overlooking the sea – or rather, the tranquil lagoon inside the reef – and my boat is rested at the dock. You should know I am very well tanned and stark naked. Inside the house I can hear the chink of ice on glass and the sound of liquor pouring. I have a sensation inside me that I can only suppose is happiness. In a moment, this quite terrific woman will appear wearing nothing much except perhaps a loosely-tied bit of fabric around her hips. She will come and stand beside me and smile and say, "Cocktail time, Bernie." I will reach up and take a glass of Mount Gaye rum – the absolutely only choice, old fruit – and tonic with ice and a slice of lime. I will set it aside and squint up at her smiling countenance and take in her wonderfully elegant teats and shapely belly. Then I will run my hand up her smooth calves, her inner thigh, until it is stopped at a soft and tactile junction. And as she lets whatever offcut of light material drop from her waist I will turn and bury my grateful face in her fragrant muff. At which she will stroke my head and hold me to herself and wriggle her hips, and call me a randy old dog, so that this is just a shared kiss between us that won't make her spill or otherwise forego her drink. Later we might take our golf cart to Jerry's Bar and drink a bottle or two of wine and eat chargrilled grouper and fries. At some point we might fuck in whatever way seems right for the mood, or even not, because there is quite possibly a tomorrow.

'Are you jealous, Bruno? You fucking should be. How many men of my age have this? I spent a lot of time with Minou in my head and how it should have been her and me. Lindy isn't Minou and never could be, but she is young, sexy and good to be with, and seems to love me, which was Minou. So I have this chance to relive the past a little. Or at least get through now, pleasantly; and after three large rums, all of it. The thing is, it's so pleasant I even get to wonder if Lindy might still like to try for a kid and wouldn't it be sexy to fuck for one so she would feel better about screwing. I mean, for after I've gone and she meets more conventional guys. Then again, as she's bought a digi-cam, I think we could make a great little movie. I don't think I am so photogenic, but the camera loves her. I think that goes for me too. Should I marry her, Bruno? Well, Bernie, my old chum, I hear you say, that's your fucking problem. We both know what she's going to say.'

Finis

Bernd, aged 6 in 1942. On the seafront at Clacton with Count Magnus.

At the house in the Boulevard St. Michel.
On the back of the photo is written 'Celine'.

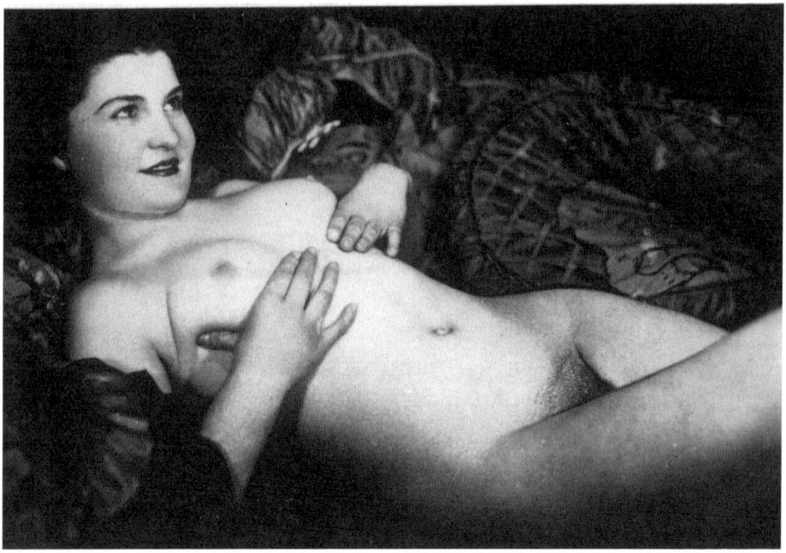

Probably taken in Hedda's Meard Street, Soho club.

Noreen, Bernd's school matron and first lover.

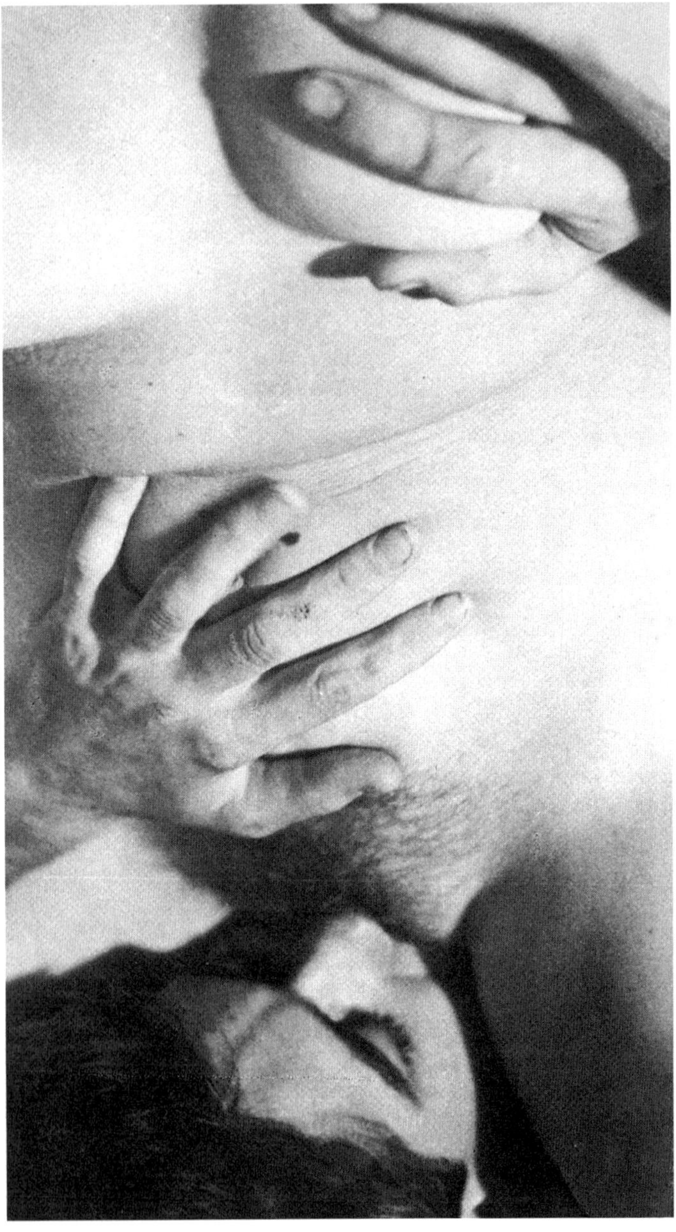

Still from the Liebe *series.*

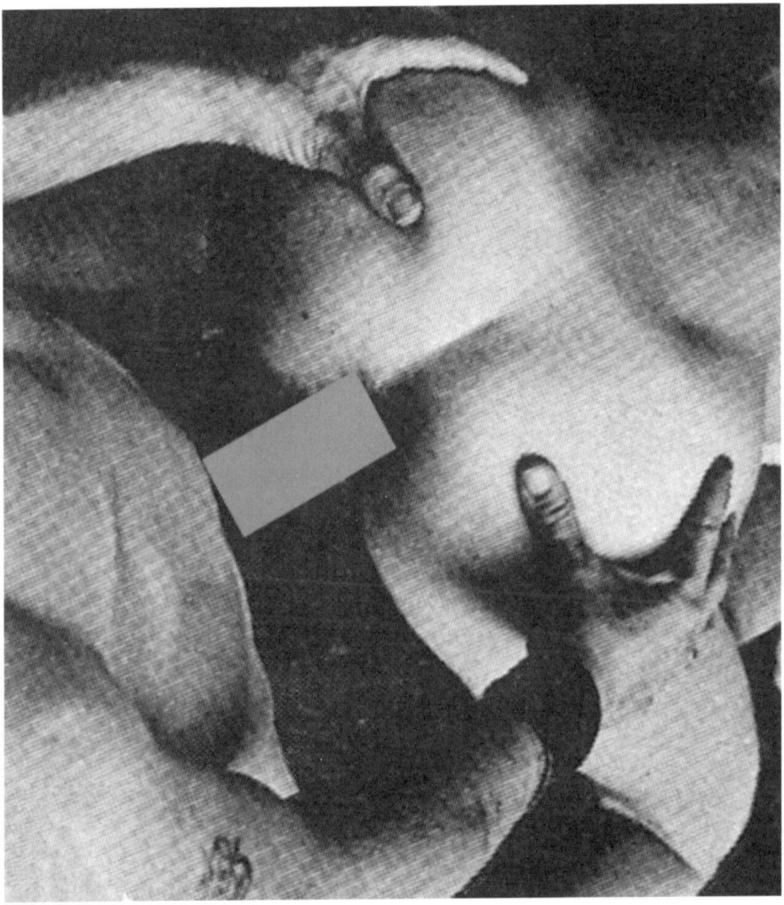

Still from the Liebe *series.*

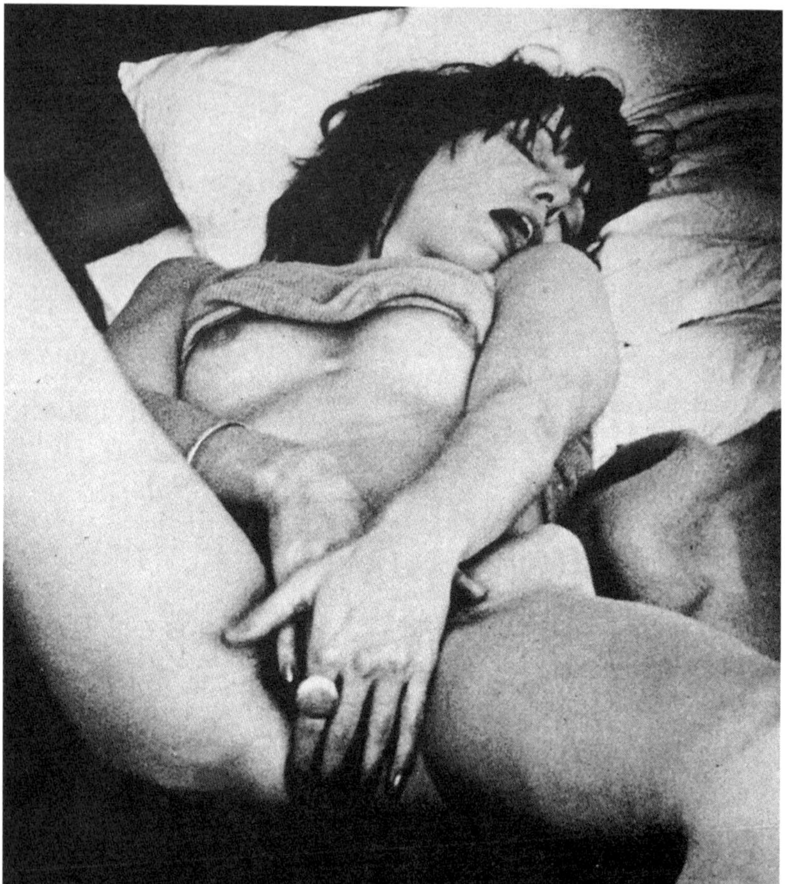

Still from the Liebe *series. A classic Töstian opening sequence.*

Hedda Töst by her lover's car
in which she was to die a short time later.

Filming Melanie.

Whilst filming Melanie, *the cast take some well-deserved time off.*

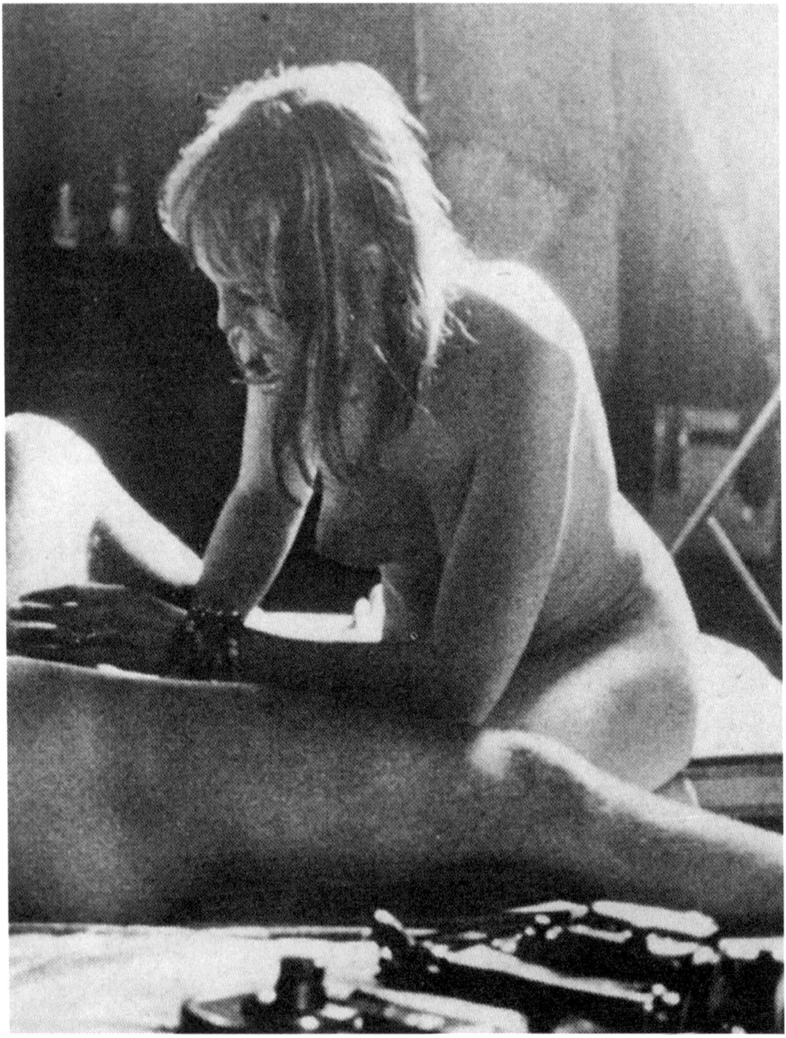

Still from Fick Alles

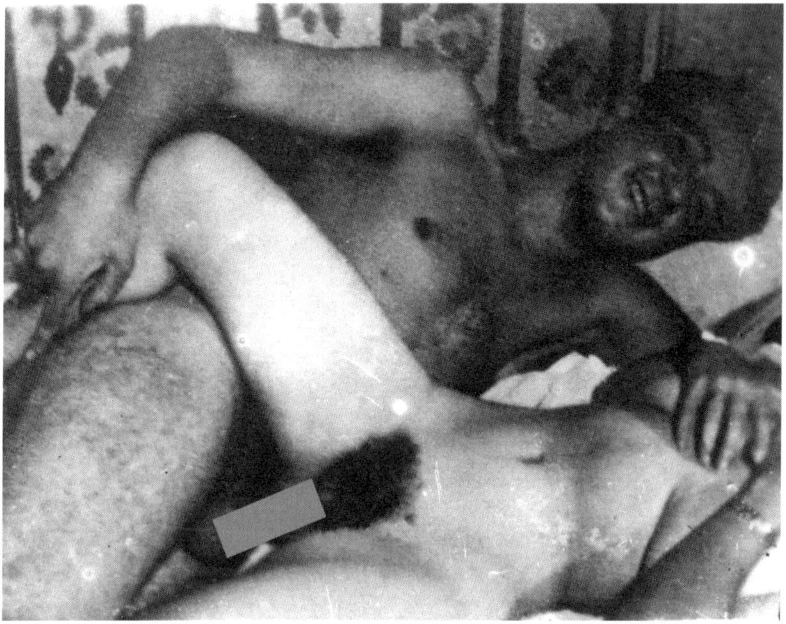

Still from Fick Alles

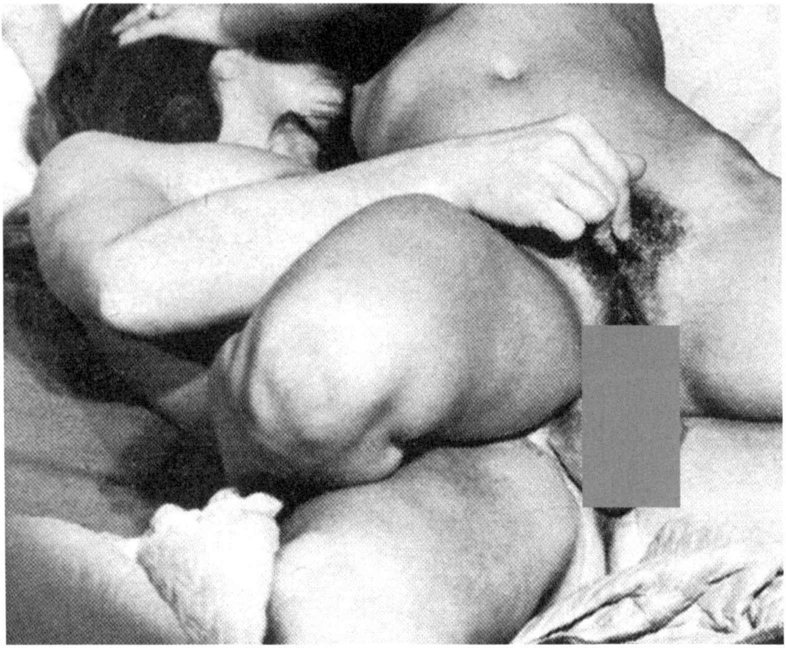

Still from Fick Alles

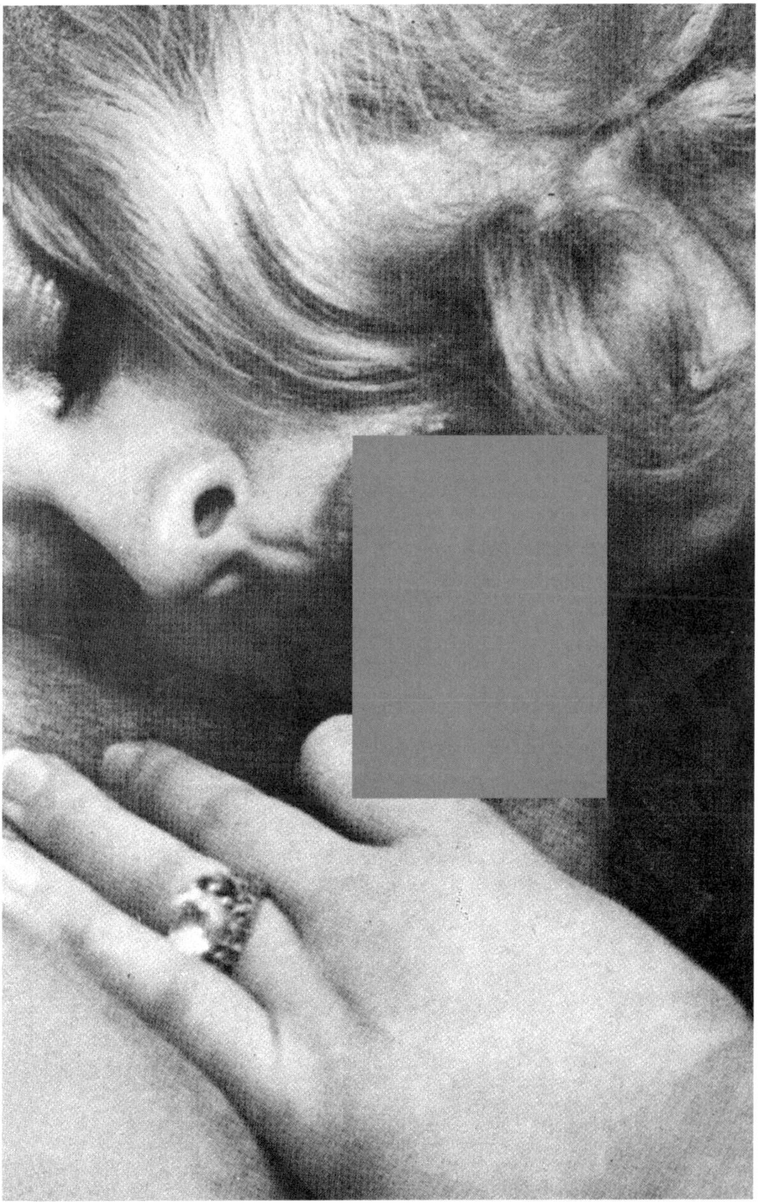

Still from The Absence of Real Desire.
The actor is possibly Cayman Montrose.

Appendix I
The *Liebe* trilogy: Bernd Töst in conversation
Blue magazine 11th April 1963

BM: Mr Töst, it's been said that these three movies are not just dirty, they're dull.
Töst: Call me Bernd. Ask any of the jerk-offs who ruined their Kleenex watching them if they're dull.

BM: You must admit they are different. An entire 75 minutes devoted to one sexual activity from virtually one camera angle; and in black and white.
Töst: Not true; except they are in black and white. There's fifteen minutes of establishment and the after-climax moments, plus a lot of time devoted to the actors' interaction, faces and gestures.

BM: But overall that is still an hour of a cock going in and out of an orifice. I'm only making this point to establish your thinking and to give you a chance to reply to your critics.

Töst: OK. I mean the first thing is that people fucking or whatever, is what the audience comes to see. They come to see it because the interaction of human genitals is of perennial interest. Why? Because everyone knows people get a big kick out of sex. If you have sex, you like being reminded, and if you don't, the pictures let you participate a little. Mostly, though, the reason I make my films the way I do, is to do with focus on the experience. I mean, sex can get awful busy and you can lose track, so when it's over you think 'That was nice,' but you can't quite remember the detail, especially when it gets near to orgasm and you're closing down on your general sensations. What I do is to take that piece of the action, which is the cock and the cunt, say, and give people a long time to appreciate the sheer sexiness of what's going on down there. It's beautiful and fascinating. Filmmakers have forgotten that. Think about a still photo of, say, some girl with a cock in her ass. You can look and look at it forever. It's hot and involving. Nowadays they just want to crank the action along and get more actors fucking everyone and it gets very confusing. It might be fun, but it's still confusing and ultimately unsatisfactory. You want to say 'Hey, slow down, let's see that again.' Now look at my films. Take *Arsch Liebe*. There's that particular angle of her half on her side, and her leg is raised so all the while you can see the cock sliding in and out and the rim of her anus gripping the shaft. You have a lot of time to watch. But you can also see her cunt and the hair and the wetness and even in black and white you get the flush of her vulva. So when you say, 'Oh, but it's just a cock and an arsehole,' you're wrong. Even more, there are those fantastic moments when her hand comes down and her fingers are splayed and she half-masturbates herself and half-feels his shaft and balls. You notice that this is partly defensive – 'Hey, take care in there,' and partly deeply sensual – she can't see but she wants to feel. Women use their hands a lot in sex. And then you look and see her face, just when the camera moves a little, or I've gone close-up. Look at her lips, her tongue, her grimaces. Then tell me there's nothing going on. I tell you, everything is going on but we're taking the time to stay focused on what is important. People can join in sensually for a long period of time and look around a small but rich territory and really appreciate why this is so enjoyable to do.

BM: We notice that in all three films you only have two actors, and they are the same two. That is, no group sex or threesomes.

Töst: True. That's because of the focus thing. It's a popular fantasy to have one woman fucking two or more men but it's hard for the audience to perceive it in other than a general way. I mean, even as director you take a medium shot, say, and there's a cock in her mouth and another in her fanny, but to make it work as a unified visual experience is damn tough. Also, it's tougher on the actors in so far as it is, how shall we say, more contrived, less easy to get lost in the action. I've done that, though; I mean, allowed the actors to just have fun. It's richer in an erotic sense, but you can lose what the producers think the audience wants – that is, just the crass directness. With *Liebe*, I tried simply to be real. Two sexy people having a great time with each other.

BM: To stay with the Liebe *trilogy, you mentioned the women's responses and facial expressions and your emphasis on those. Men in your movies seem much more anonymous.*
Töst: [laughing] I'm a man and I like women better. No, to be serious, Mae West said, 'What is a man but a cock.' Well, I don't entirely agree, but in this case she has a point. Women are very aesthetic, cat-like creatures and their reactions are complex and interesting. Also, a man in close-up, say, performing cunnilingus as in *Fotze Liebe*, is very hard to film sensually. I was lucky in finding the right man, who was with the girl, I mean, her lover, and he was terrific. He was young and had a great complexion and hardly needed to shave and a good body – neat ass and so forth. He looked great licking the girl out because, actually, he looked somewhat like a girl himself. Also, he and the girl were very good together sexually so this was why I saw no reason to change.

BM: Is it also that most of your audience are men?
Töst: Not really. They are, but that is more the producers' and distributors' problem. I would love for more women to enjoy my movies. In fact, I think more women would like to enjoy pornography if the material and the social approval thing allowed. Actually, I think women are perfectly OK with the explicit. But, like I said, they are more complicated maybe and need slightly different cues and references; not just this romance and foreplay crap, simply to recognise how they see things. I mean, *O* was written by a woman.

BM: Is this why you chose to have a man's perspective for Fotze *and a woman's for* Schwanz*?*
Töst: In part, maybe. Mainly though it was just realistic. I mean, women like cocks almost as much as men. That is, men think their dicks are fantastic, and women like a good penis too. It made sense to work with the way a woman sees the cock in her life at that moment when she's got it out and up and is fully engaged. With cunts it's different. I think both sexes are ambivalent about the vagina. I wanted to demonstrate what a glorious place it is. It's not just a hole that leaks and is good for shoving your cock into, it's a major piece of sexual engineering that looks good, feels good, tastes good and does you good.

BM: There are long periods in these films when there is virtually no sound at all. Just breathing, and the sounds of sex. Why did you reject sound effects or even music?
Töst: Obviously because that's artificial as a directorial construct. My actors can play music, have a football game on the TV, say dirty things to each other, or just grunt if they want to. Or they can simply get on with fucking – their choice. Let's face it, going, 'Yes, baby, oh yes, fuck me, fuck my ass, fuck my mouth,' may or may not be what people say in real life. If it's faked for the movie the audience will know. If you want dialogue, write some decent dialogue. I've never had my actors saying anything quite as banal as I've just exemplified, allowing for the fact that, in

the circumstances, no one quotes Tennyson. They whisper sweet nothings and say, 'Oh, sweetie, that feels good,' and they may go, 'Oh fuck me, give it to me,' when they are coming. Otherwise they just smooch stickily away in their own idiom, and their own language too.

BM: All three films were notable for the way they treated orgasm, in that the actors came at the same time and you spent some time dwelling on the build toward actual moment of ejaculation and its aftermath. You even reprise specific shots.

Töst: The standard cum shot usually infers that the woman has either come already or gets her kicks from the guy jerking off over her. There's a squirt of greater or lesser volume for obvious reasons and cut to it in situ and away. My people come together because that's high-quality sex. Plus you get the reality, stiff teats, real moaning and so forth. I also insisted for this that there was no orgasm for the previous 24 hours. That has its problems, but again, makes for better sex. Last, it is the climactic moment. It's not just him using her, it's her enjoying him too. It's a fun thing to have your lover shoot over or in you. If it isn't, why are you having sex and why am I filming it? So let's spend time on it and look at all this hairiness and juice and the sticky minutes, however they occur, provided it was natural. Yes, the reprise is contrived, and is a bit of film technique but why not? Porn is too cynical and too quick, it aims to dissatisfy not to satisfy.

BM: Bernd, this has been a real pleasure. There are so many other things we'd like to talk about but maybe another day?
Töst: My pleasure.

Note: *Blue* magazine went bust in 1968 and its editor played a key role in setting up *Screw* magazine.

Appendix 2
Meeting the stars
– interviews with surviving actors

Nearly thirty years have gone by since Töst's last movie. Death, the desire for anonymity and the fact that most of the cast worked under stage names, has made it hard to catch up with more than a few alumni. The publishers managed it, however, and one Spring day, in the Plaza Hotel Manhattan, five of Töst's actors sat round a table in a private room and talked about the man and his movies.

With us, and under names that may or may not be really theirs, were:

Helga Divine: the star of *Fick Alles*. Helga is a slim, stylish woman in her fifties and still in the sex business. She is proprietor of a chain of sex clubs and cinemas based in Hamburg.

Dieter Ulm: the young actor in the *Liebe* trilogy. Dieter had a brief career with Lasse Braun after his Töst debut, but gave it up when he married one of his fellow actors and is now a luxury car dealer in Munich.

Rosita Dumarnier: played Sophie in *Melanie*. Rosita has put on a little weight – she says – but still looks good and is a happily married mother of three grown children. She lives – mostly – in Nice.

CAYMAN MONTROSE: was one of the heroines of *The Absence of Real Desire.* She is, she says, 'pleasantly divorced' and runs a real estate business in Fort Lauderdale.

RALPH FAIRFAX: the ingénue hero of *The Sick Room.* He lives in London where he has three very successful brasserie bars. He has been married twice and is currently single.

Dieter: You know, it's amazing to be here. Actually, Helga and I still keep in touch from time to time. Luckily my wife was in the same business so there is no problem (laughs).
Helga: He even sold me a Mercedes – at a good price.
Ralph: I wouldn't have missed this for anything. I've seen all Bernd's films and it is a privilege to be with you all. I think we all stayed up too late last night talking about Bernd and doing those films. I was never ashamed of it, but you don't go round boasting either.
Rosita: How true that is. It took me a lot of courage to tell my husband. That was when we became engaged. By then, I had stopped films; I only made three or four and was doing modelling. Anyway, he was very sweet and says he fancied Melanie, the bad man. We haven't told the kids and we lost the film copy we had.
Cayman: Yeah, you were lucky. I had a tough time

living down that *Desire* movie. All I got offered was really sleazy loops. Then *Playboy* picked me up and was real nice and I made good money just doing soft stuff and then I got *Baywatch* for a season. No, that and the divorce did me real well. I loved Bernd though. He was a gentleman.

So let's talk about Bernd. You all seem to like him. Why?

Helga: Respect; he respected us, he respected the work. He liked the business and it showed. Some directors they are ashamed, or they despise the actors or maybe themselves.

Rosita: He was funny, he laughed a lot. Though he could be unpredictable.

Ralph: He also made it easy for us to get it on together. I mean, however horny you are, when there's a crew and a set you need to feel comfortable.

Cayman: Well, that's generally true in the business. I think it was partly just his style, but also he really had a point of view, a story or something he felt strongly about.

Dieter: Yes, I found that. You believed you were not just a body or a stud but an actor. He said to me: 'A cock is easy to find. I want the person it belongs to.'

Rosita: You know, right from the first meeting, like at the casting, he made you feel good, sexy even. I'd come from nude modelling – you know, the 'hey babe, give it to me' type of thing. Bernd just

shook your hand and started to talk about the film and what sort of things I found sexy and so on.
Helga: What you say is right – then he says, well, what I have in mind is…
Cayman: Yes, and by the time he's finished you're feeling horny as all hell.
Dieter: I noticed that, but with us he was always pleasant but much more, how do I say, practical.
Ralph: Maybe because he could see we were looking at the girls and going, oh boy, am I a lucky guy. (They all laugh.)
Cayman: Actually I think there is a serious point there. He knew we would perform better if we had motivation; the guys needed it less.
Ralph: I think that's a bit unfair; everyone benefits from feeling there's a purpose.
Cayman: OK, I agree, but we girls had a tad more psyching up to do if we were to make it real. Bernd was good at that, which is why his movies still hold up.

They were and are good, yet they seemed not quite to make it as sex films or serious ones. You've seen them all now, what do you think?
Helga: It's a combination of a very reserved market and economics. Plus Bernd refused to compromise.
Rosita: I like some more than others. I thought *Fick Alles* was very brilliant and you were wonderful in it, Helga, but it was not sexy. It was a very tough story and I think you had to be rather perverted

to feel aroused. *Super Bitch* I liked because it respected women but again, not sexy. (Helga nods and pats Rosita's hand.)

Cayman: Did you find *Melanie* sexy when you watched it again yesterday?

Rosita: Oh yes, but I found it sexy to make, so some good memories came back.

Helga: I think this shows how good a director Bernd was. Objectively I agree, *FA* is not a sexy movie, but to do it was exciting. I won't say sexy, but it was sexually arousing. Maybe it was something in the story and in me about control.

Ralph: Well, this probably explains why he didn't get more successful – people found it hard to work out where he was coming from.

Dieter: I think this is so. Like anything, people have certain expectations and the product has to follow rules. Sometimes you can break them but it is high risk.

Helga: I once told Dieter that, having seen him in the *Liebe* trilogy, I thought he would be a fine lover.

Dieter: Thank you. It was a good film to make. I had lots of help though.

Cayman: I have to agree with Helga. I think the whole series is very sexually arousing. Speaking as a woman, I felt he'd put real affection into the explicit.

Rosita: I think it was amazing that Bernd was only 24 and these were his first serious films.

Ralph: That's the point, they are serious films.

The dirty movie boys don't want serious and they don't want attitude.

As you've mentioned audiences, how do, or did, you feel about the people who watch you in your films?
Cayman: That's very cleverly put. Personally, I felt nothing. It certainly didn't affect my performance. I take my clothes off, have sex or wave my fanny at the camera, dress and go home. That is, I used to. (Laughs.)
Helga: As someone still in the business I can share quite a lot of what Cayman says. To be honest, I try not to think about it because then you start to dislike your customer and that is not good.
Rosita: I used to like to think of handsome boys getting off on pictures of me in their bedroom, but I didn't like thinking too much about, shall we say, the men in sex shops.
Cayman: Yeah, oddly I didn't mind thinking about men in hotel rooms, though really you try not to visualise too much.
Ralph: I feel sorry for guys who have no other outlet for their sex drive. I don't like the exploitation that goes on in many aspects of the sex trade. I don't care who watched me, though it would have been nice if girls had come up to me in the street and begged to see my cock!
Dieter: You mean, they didn't? (Laughter.)
Helga: Thinking back, you know, about *FA*, I wanted men to go out of the cinema or finish watching, and feel stunned and bad about

themselves and more respectful of women and wanting to change things. Men have to behave in my clubs and I will not have violent things against women even as a joke. Bernd made me think deeply about these matters. Before that, I just fucked a lot and didn't care who watched.

Cayman: That's very honest. I was too flip earlier. In truth, I got a kick out of showing off my body in *Playboy* and so forth. *Absence of Desire* wasn't so much about the audience as about me. The audience in my mind were to be made to go, 'Oh my God.' When I saw that film again yesterday – the first time since I made it, by the way – I was wiped out. When we did it, it was, in truth, fun. I liked sex, the boys were easy to get on with off set and it was all a gas. But when I see it now, I realise that I was a totally sleazy nymphomaniac and just what men wanted to see, with their cock in their hand. I can only suppose the movie was too intelligent for a mass audience of jerk-offs, to their loss. Still, I think I can be proud of my performance in a weird way. I had only done a couple of things and was starting to think about 'why' and the meaning of things – including sex.

Rosita: I think we can all be proud. You know, I never really admitted this even to myself, but I deeply enjoyed being Sophie. Partly it was so different to how I saw myself. I was quite a bourgeois little girl and sex was my rebellion. Sophie's total sexual abandon was thrilling. In fact, I think the lesbian scenes were just as exciting as anything.

For a while, until I was married, I was bisexual in my private life too. I liked the film then and I still do. I wonder where Lorraine is now?
Dieter: This is getting away from Bernd, isn't it?
Ralph: Maybe not; at least he made fuck films that had relevance for us.

It's OK to talk about yourselves. I get the feeling that Bernd tapped into something for you people and that is part of the story?
Dieter: Well, you know, we must be careful not to make things too general. I mean, none of us had very long in the sex business – except Helga and she doesn't act in or produce films any more. We were all recruited young and if we were not innocents we were not sex movie pros. What is more, we got out pretty quickly.
Ralph: That's fair. I mean, fourteen years separate Dieter and me but he and I agree that nothing much seems to have changed in the basics. Porn stuff is just another way to earn a living. I think the pros were – still are mostly – good people. They didn't need to make a big thing out of fucking or whatever. I mean, the girl who was the under-matron, oh wow, did I fall for her. She was cute, sweet to me and sexy as all hell. The whole thing was brilliant. I said to her, 'Do you get sexed up doing this?' She said 'Oh yes, especially if the man is attractive and we have a rapport. If not, I fake it like all women. Anyway it's not marriage or nursing and I'm too lazy to be a scientist.'

Dieter: Ralph is so right. Julie, my sex-partner in *Liebe* I had met in Copenhagen. We had an extraordinary affair, which we just took onto the set. When we first met she told me she had worked in a house in Paris where they had orgies. Frankly, I was somewhat inexperienced but she was so nice to me. She said, 'Do you like a girl's conillon?' I said I did. She said, 'Good, then it means we can enjoy. I will tell you how I like mine to be pleased.' And she told me and it was very useful and also sexy and made us good friends. Bernd said he was very happy with our physical rapport – but in truth, Julie led everything.
Helga: But you didn't marry her.
Dieter: No, Helga, as you know very well. Julie went off with an Italian aristocrat and Anna-Marie and I just fell in love with each other on one of Lasse's shoots and that was our last sex film. Now he was a good man too in his way and less complex than Bernd.
Cayman: I'm intrigued. You guys seem to be saying that you accidentally got into the sex film business, met two girls who were nice to you, had some good fucks, got married and left.
Dieter: Pretty much.
Ralph: The nice girls bit is right. I first married what the English mean by a nice girl with several hundred acres of Gloucestershire who preferred riding horses to me.
Cayman: That's not fair. We girls have been through psychological trauma about our sexual

identity, been fucked and squirted over countless times and still bear the scars.
Ralph: But you made the choices and yourself said it was an important part of your life.
Cayman: So I did (laughs). Plus, there were some fun and sexy people.
Dieter: Don't forget, the girls always got paid much better.
Rosita: Rightly so.
Helga: Not always.

How do you want to sum up this get-together and your memories of Bernd Töst?
Dieter: The meeting has been great. I hope we shall stay in touch. Bernd is a pleasant memory for me. He was a nice guy with a certain talent in a business that has some of those qualities; and equally some talentless shits.
Ralph: I support that. Bernd may not be the greatest unsung film hero but he tried hard, and was interesting, and for me it was a truly pleasurable education.
Helga: My career has been better because of him. He helped me to fight my demons without too much pain. This discussion has been interesting. In reality, Bernd was not and is not the only sex film director to try for at least the actors' well-being. Many do not but many do. His work does deserve a better respect though because I do feel it has some content. I think he did good porn but *FA* was really a non-porn film.

Rosita: I think a little piece of my past has been properly resolved. I am so glad we have met and I think of you now as my friends. It is time for me to take my souvenir DVD copy of *Melanie* home and leave it for my children to find. For this, and for his nice manners, I am glad of Bernd.
Cayman: Rosita says it for me. I want a copy of all the movies, not just mine, and I'm going to ring up this guy who thinks he wants to marry me and say: 'If you don't like this, you don't get me.' And my message to Bernd is simply – 'Good going, sweetie.'

Having met, do you wish you had made a film together?
(Silence and smiles.)
Helga: If we had, it would have been great but we did what we did. By the way, Ralph, I met your nurse from your film, in Japan. Sonja and I will possibly have a business deal, I'll tell you about her if you like...

Appendix 3
Töst the film maker – a synopsis of key work

Overall, Töst's output as a commercial 'shorts' pornographic filmmaker must have been huge. Most often, however, he refused credits and the few that have survived must be regarded as jobbing work. Those reviewed hereunder stand for Töst as auteur.

The Liebe Series, 1958, 16mm B/w, 3 x 75mins

This trilogy has already been discussed in some detail - notably in the *Blue* magazine interview. It should be noted, however, that Andy Warhol tacitly acknowledged Töst's influence on his own moviemaking, not least in focus at great length on specifics and the repetition of key images. What is also interesting is that despite the period in which they were made – the late 1950s – it is quite hard to date them from the set or the actor's hairstyle and clothing. Apart from the close-up treatment, in these films Töst favoured French Empire style bedheads and related visible accoutrements (an echo of Rue Madeleine?). He also always liked his actors to look natural, even dishevelled, if female, but always neat in their bodily presentation, especially men. Therefore he hated moustaches, too tidy or too unkempt hair and too much make-up. 'I like the mascara and the lipstick to blur under the impact of lust,' he once said. 'Give sex a chance to sweat.' His liking for 16mm and ability with lighting meant also that not only was the contrast and texture excellent –

compared to, say, the favoured Super-8mm of the day – but the films have lent themselves very well to digitalisation. We are lucky that, even though he was not a very good businessman, Töst's devotion to film and quality meant that he hung on to some of his master prints and refused to sell them off even when very poor. We should remember that Töst was only 24 when he made these films. His assurance is amazing.

Melanie, 1963, 16mm Colour, 90mins

The title itself tells us that something else was going on at this time. Töst was still a young man. He had served his apprenticeship, made money, fought and won battles and clearly wanted to take his art a stage further. Some argue that this film was the progenitor of as diverse sex films as *Beyond the Valley of the Dolls*, *The Green Door*, *The Devil in Miss Jones*, *Misty Beethoven*, *Emmanuelle*, and even *Debbie Does Dallas* – though this last stretches credulity. The directors of these movies have never acknowledged any debt. Töst himself, when asked, simply shrugged and said: 'Who knows, those are other people's films.' Töst had also done nothing except hack work for the preceding five years. As has been previously noted, the influence of his sister and, in effect, partner Minou, was acknowledged by Töst, not least in the use of her given name for the title. How much their love affair was reflected in the choice of title remained part of a forbidden territory for discussion.

Whatever the case, *Melanie* is unique, arguably a first in explicit film, which it would be hard not to see as influential. When released into the awkward, if developing, market, which was the USA of its time and a variable European climate, it nonetheless rewarded the producer's faith in his director. Despite the dreadful technology of the era, the 16mm format gave it great appeal in the club cinema and private audience sector. Super-8 adaptations and the Far East added to sales. Töst – who had from pride rather than commercial judgement put his own money into the production – probably earned the modern equivalent of $500,000 from it, twenty times the fee he got for the *Liebe* series. Compared to the earnings of modern pornographic videos and their directors, this was very good indeed. Whilst only enjoying a comeback in rather limited circles of erotic appreciation, *Melanie* is apparently playing to large audiences in the newly liberal Baltic States and Töst's 'native' and porn-weary Denmark.

Of this film, Töst would only say: 'It cost a lot to make, and it is too elaborate but there are some individually great moments. It was a time when I craved acceptance and felt powerful enough to challenge the mainstream. Minou was very keen to have more sophistication, complexity and emotional content. So I confused sex and art. Then I came to know what I had always known. Sex is Art. Still, Min had a point, the movie made real money.'

More kindly, William Heifetz – a rather courageous reviewer for *Atlantic* magazine, in admitting he had seen a blue movie – wrote: 'That the main aim of this film must be to titillate the sexual appetite – to put it at its most delicate – is unarguable. Nonetheless, it has at least an idea of narrative and a passing belief that context and perception have a relationship to each other and to the sexual act. The heroine may, at first glance, be dismissed as no better than a whore, but is she any worse than the celebrated courtesans of the past? She is certainly more liberated, more full of character and less cypher-like than the men in her life.'

Mr Heifetz's reason for reviewing the film was that there was much debate, at the time both in the USA and Britain, about the law and pornography, obscenity and freedom of speech. He had essentially taken it to illustrate a point about the legitimising effect of context and character. Töst, of course, took precisely the opposing view.

The eponymous heroine is first seen, in an uncharacteristic piece of situation embellishment, walking down the street to the admiration of various working men. It is short, nicely done, and in a perfectly modern way, uses the opportunity both to arouse interest and run the key titles. Thereafter, the film follows its heroine through a developing series of sexual encounters that are partly fantasy and partly real. The clue is a slight optical effect to suggest 'reality' shifting to a different set of events that may be imaginary or part of her sexual history. The plot seems to suggest initially a sexy girl alert to men's fantasies, and also a woman disappointed in love and cynical about men. Then follows a spontaneous one-night stand with a neighbour, a lesbian encounter, sibling incest and a descent into general sexual abandonment. For those keen for a happy ending, Töst provides one. Melanie, her lesbian lover and her incestuous brother settle down happily in the country with a circle of like-minded dissolutes.

The evidence is that, apart from the opening shot in Manhattan somewhere and some perfectly anonymous apartments, Töst was able to persuade his distributor – though his personal financial commitment must have helped – to let him rent the genuine French manoir where the main sexual action occurs.

With the advantage of inside knowledge it is obvious that Bernd and Minou were externalising their relationship. It may also be that the whole film is Töst working out his feelings about women. In Hedda, Noreen and Minou he had had some rather unusual examples of the gender. The filmed Melanie is an ambivalent personality, in sexual and other terms. Her motivations seem entirely hedonistic in that she will fuck anyone at the slightest provocation. Yet she seems to be searching and her brother is at the heart of it. Töst is recorded as having said when asked about not being married: 'I don't know what being married is really about. I had a mother and a sister I adored. They were wonderful to me and to be with. Other women have been charming in my life and I have no difficulty in finding a partner to fuck with. Marriage is such a lottery, but your mother, brother or sister is to some extent you.'

Whatever, this is a sex film, though perhaps not quite a film about sex, as Bernd would have wished, and Melanie – together with her friends – has, well, a ball.

The film does, however, have one last interesting subtext and this is to do with Töst's treatment of sexual violence and S&M themes. He made no secret of his distaste for – or what he later called lack of empathy for – both homosexual as well as sado-masochistic acts. 'If that's what people like, fine,' he once said, 'but if I can't feel the excitement I can't film it so well.' In fact, he dealt with both forms of sexual activity in *Melanie* and elsewhere. But it is clear from the context in this film how he viewed these matters. Whether his willingness to film such scenes came from intellectual honesty, artistic integrity or merely commercial reality, we shall never know. They certainly recurred as elements of later movies, as did other controversial themes including rape, incest and under age sex.

Suffice it to say that there is an interesting group sex encounter. In this, Melanie – who is very much the 'point de vue' – engages in cunnilingus with her lesbian lover who is being sodomised by her – the lover's – male sibling who in turn is being buggered by a male consort. The power of the encounter, which also involves bisexual fellatio and ejaculation, is nonetheless seen not as an overt eroticisation of male congress, but 'merely', if that term can be used, as part of a general rout in which any and all genitalia are to be enjoyed. Töst agreed that these scenes owed something to de Sade, but in a somewhat defensive tone, observed, 'Goethe said there are no new ideas.'

On the S&M front, both of Melanie's encounters are fantasies. In one, she cruelly punishes her fickle lover for his infidelity. It is a pretty extreme piece of work insofar as the bondage, the beating, the forced masturbation and the final humiliation of being urinated on are forcefully realistic. In another, she fantasises a blasphemously dramatised masturbation in a church followed by a whipping and multiple sodomy. Whilst she protests the early assaults on her orifices, she quickly submits herself to pleasure.

Compared to a serious BDSM movie, however, this is not over-heavy material, and leaves the movie as a more romantic – if that is the word – work in the genre, albeit one that is classier than most before or since. Later films, notably *Fick Alles* and, more marginally, *Super Bitch* and *The Sick Room* deal more centrally with the raw outer edges of sexual experience and have also returned to his minimalist ideas.

Melanie, however, shows all the signs of becoming quite a popular classic. The sex shops of the UK and elsewhere won't stock it because it is too arty. But if ever the commercial rental companies stock sexually explicit movies, this could be one of the bestsellers.

Fick Alles, 1965, 16MM B/W, 85MINS

Fuck Everything, in its English title, is to anglophone sex films what *Das Boot* is to *Sink the Bismarck*. It is also quite evidently a reaction to Minou's defection. Whether one of revenge or despair it is not possible to know. Töst himself says, 'I wanted to get back to a simpler, purer narrative line. Sex films were becoming very mass production in feel; no style, no sensuality. Or, in the fringes of the market, they were just gross. Also frankly, there was something going on in Germany – socially, historically – in the sex industry. The kultur was weird.'

FA as he called it took him back to his roots and into quite unconventional territory. He put his own money into the project again, fearing that his US distributors might not like the film. He did however secure a promise of German and, from that, European continental distribution. Three more years of routine sex loops in New York had been enough.

'Melanie' has given way to 'Inga'. Where Melanie was soft and rounded and womanly, Inga is lean and sharp-edged with cat's eyes and a small, pointy nose and chin. In fact she is a carbon copy of the actor who played Melanie's lover Sophie in that movie. For analysts seeking to read into this, references to Minou may be right in physical terms. Since critics of pornography often aver that the genre is really homoerotic, given the emphasis on the penis, Töst has taken quite a risk with this film. The men seem to be chosen not primarily for their phallic competence and personal appearance, but for their rather harsh and threatening quality, which includes in one case penile deformity. In some respects *FA* is almost an anti-pornographic film.

The storyline is to be inferred and the action takes place pretty much in apparently authentic locations. Chiefly, a bleak room in one of post-war Berlin's bomb-damaged housing estates, and the bedroom of a modern, smart, chain hotel. There are other scenes including a cellar, the back of a Mercedes and a bombed site. All seem to involve Inga using her sexuality both to earn an immediate crust and to manipulate a situation. Her lovers include a hierarchy of wealth and influence [fatter, smart hotel, Mercedes] through power [leaner, nastier, more manipulative] into simply transactional [sleazy and hairy].

But, as Inga lends, sells, submits or otherwise exploits her body in an economical narrative that gives full scope to the sexual action, we perceive other riches of subtlety. This movie was made only three years before the Paris riots. It was made during a cold war coupled with an environment of cultural freedom in the frontier-city that was Berlin. There were mini-skirts and the pill and, on the continent, the potent mix of repression and revolution. The Bader Meinhof group were nascent. In *FA*, Töst captured all the alienation, anomie and money hunger that enveloped not only Berlin, but many other capitals at this time.

Inga allows the fat businessmen to masturbate over her in the smart hotel. She gives a blow job in the Mercedes. She spends quite a lot of time fucking her paymaster and his girlfriend and others in his sterile apartment. She has a truly horrifying, powerfully filmed time with several assailants on a bombsite. The supposition here is that some kind of assignation had been arranged with a sexual promise, but the meeting had been subverted into gang rape. It is a very difficult sequence to watch. It is graphic, and brilliant in its evocation of uncontrolled male lust. It is also intensely sensual.

Töst seems to challenge us to deal with the horror of the rape and the unbidden but real voyeuristic frisson of the fantasy. The – literally in every sense – climactic moment begins as Inga is penetrated for the third or fourth time from the rear and in both orifices, sprawled across a dumped sofa. The camera reminds you as you see her body and the pumping rapist that she has a gun under her belly. What makes her a good actress in this context, and Töst a good director, is that you understand both her submission and her relish – even sense of pleasure – in anticipation of her revenge. As the last man rises to his feet, she rolls over, gun in hand, and shoots each one of her tormentors. It is an extraordinary moment – not least in a porn film. As a character, the survivor female with edge, this makes Inga a very modern character. She anticipates many contemporary female heroes, not least of all Sigourney Weaver's Ripley in *Alien*.

Töst has also imbued her with a darker quality, one that almost seems to promise retribution to men. Inga's general demeanour is one of sullen hostility. She appears to take little pleasure from her sexual encounters, other than the perfunctory courtesy necessary to gain her aims. In that, she faithfully enacts the dissimulations of her sex. However, there are two moments when she does seem genuinely aroused: in a lesbian *soixante-neuf* embrace in which her lover is also being sodomised – a reprise on *Melanie*? – and the moment after the gang-bang when she kneels up and produces the automatic pistol, which she uses to shoot her assailants. In this latter moment her lips part, her tongue flickers sensually; we see that her nipples are engorged and she smiles – sardonically, but with an almost post-coital satisfaction. But, of course, in the bombsite case, it could just be the cold.

> 'The Iron Curtain in the East, and the pressures of totalitarian male rule everywhere give real poignancy to the idea that women must sell their sexuality to gain influence – that can be OK, if not often and only when the woman is completely in control. In the context of this film, gross as it is, there is an idea, which spells out every feisty girl's feminine power and revenge fantasy.' – Ellen Mendez, feminist writer, *Nova* magazine, 1971.

> 'As a story we perceive only that Inga is one tough girl who is trying to get oppression out and freedom in. Sex is the key, death the exit. Inga is therefore the inheritor of, say, Boudicca and the antecedent of twenty-first century computer and TV queens (Lara Croft, Buffy, Xena), who represent strong women who deal in sex and death.' – Dee Mcdonald for *Playboy*.

Erotic or the obverse, we cannot deny the essential toughness and nihilism of this movie. Stripped of the explicit sex it might have had the impact of *Knife in the Water*. As it stands, with the dominance of the – arguably exploitative – sexual element, it still has power. In fact, the sex tells us stuff no other films do. It is raw and uncompromising. Inga's experience of sex is that of the alley cat. Töst said of this movie: 'Some people say I'm just exploiting women and sex. I say it went on. It goes on. There's nothing here to pervert truth. No one is asked to get their rocks off on rape and abuse. I have no recall of what I was trying to say. It was just a sexy woman who could use her body to get a result. Sometimes you win, sometimes you lose. Inga was a winner. The so-called gang-bang rape was involuntary, but she knew how to be fucked and she knew she had the pay-off. That was sweet for her. Yes, I went back to this weird country and these truly sexually and economically strange girls. It struck me then that there were stories to be told and that this was a good place and the right time. Probably it was about fucking the revolution into being and better achieved by taking the squirt in the cunt than the bullet in the head. Like everything else, the fun option often loses in real life. So, give hope a chance.'

Super Bitch in the Halls of the Sex Warriors, 1969, 35MM COLOUR, 105MINS

This is an extraordinary work in many ways, and the first time Töst came close to directing a more mainstream movie. It is shot in 35mm, and clearly had a quite substantial budget. There was an unproven rumour that Larry Flint's *Hustler* magazine may have commissioned or backed it. What is certain is that Töst cut a sanitised version, which became more generally promoted. The film achieved wide cable distribution – cut and uncut – in the USA and can still be seen occasionally on some hotel adult channels around the world, except the UK.

The movie is set in a brothel, somewhere in the desert – implicitly, Nevada and near Las Vegas. There is every reason to believe that this is a real brothel and that at least some of the girls are genuine whores. They may also have had porn film experience, of course. Whether the clientele are for real or actors is much harder to decide. Bernd insists they were real johns. If so, they are remarkably relaxed in the camera's presence.

Super Bitch is, of course, the ruling madam and the girls are her sex warriors. It's a witty title and sets the movie's thesis quite explicitly. Töst admires and loves these women, whom he sees as keeping secure the sexual boundaries of society. The customers, however regarded – and Töst's camera remains more or less neutral in that matter – would clearly be at least a nuisance and often a danger, to themselves and others, were their lusts not managed by our heroines.

Töst's direction, the lighting and the use of 35mm create a visual effect that is close to Impressionist painting – and Renoir specifically. In narrative terms we simply move from room to room as the several and varied encounters of the girls' day occur. Sometimes these are social and in public areas – the bars, lounges and swimming pool. At other times they are in private rooms, whether the girl's personal quarters or the service bedrooms, as they are called. The impact is remarkable in what might structurally seem like a pretty flat documentary.

Each location is framed and held exactly like a painting, but it is a painting in which the subjects move and time passes. Medium shot is used for groups, and tight parallel and often overhead for the more intimate scenes. Töst uses considerable artifice in the way his female subjects are presented. Hairstyles, make-up and, in many regards, clothing, are quite explicit in their reference to fin de siècle France. There is much use of cami-knickers, bustiers and very feminine frothy garter belts and other accoutrements. Leather and rubber wear is what it is, but even here, the dominatrices – led by Madame – keep a period feel, if only through the high-heeled lace-up boots.

Töst lets his camera observe the girls fondly and unobtrusively as they use their skills to relax and pleasure clients, chatter with each other or take quiet time out for their rest and recuperation. At times it is hard to tell if he is in the room, but of course he is, as very subtle, almost imperceptible adjustments to focal length – but not angle – tell us. When we have spent a good time as it were with the cameo, to absorb its detail as in a gallery, we move on through the simple, yet effective device of a brief fade and refocus.

The narrative as such simply follows the day from dawn and awakening to the small hours and the last girls' retreat to their own bedrooms. The film is silent in that there is no audible dialogue. Instead all one hears is the murmur of voices, whoever is talking. Sometimes there is muzak. The meaning and the context come entirely from the facial expressions of the protagonists. The girls emerge as simply rather charming working women. They have personalities, of course, and off-duty the mask can slip in a grimace of dislike, a slight sag of tiredness. On duty they are bright and smiling – or as aggressively raunchy or demurely submissive as the situation demands. Even Madame, the Super Bitch – clearly as tough as a marine sergeant – is more like a Mother Superior to her charges.

So, what do we make of the clients? Töst is non-judgemental about their sexual preferences, but they are merely ciphers, ghosts – almost irrelevant as people. They present in various shapes and sizes. Their clothing is anonymous, and one realises it is the same. Töst has dressed them all in white shirts, with or without check sport jacket, black or beige trousers, ditto loafers and, for the record, white jockey shorts. They appear in and leave the shot unremarked. Their presence is as a penis or a pair of buttocks, occasionally as a face or a whole body but then only when the attire and its attendant fantasy require it. Only in one case, where the client wished to whip his hostess, is a face shown for long. It is salutary. There on a rather weak but vicious face we see an expression both of relish and shame. It is not nice. Indeed, we can question this film's place in the canon of pornography. In general, it paints a rather depressing picture of male sexual fantasy, both in its limited range of expression and the all too frequent anti- rather than fulfilled climax.

This is not to say that the encounters themselves are without pleasure for the clients. The girls fellate, masturbate, whip, fondle, urinate on, gasp at, and all the other things required by the clients with a relaxed and underlying good humour. There are limits. No swallowing semen, no coprophiliac activity at all other than conventional anal sex, no urination on the girl – though the man can take it where he likes. Male domination cannot go further than the girl allows and they will not permit blood to be drawn. The movie is sexy only where you as viewer might identify with the activity. It is however very sexy indeed when we see our heroines at leisure, unclothed or dressed, being women alone or together. There is also a wonderful comic moment when we are observing a girl masturbating a man who is watching a pornographic film. This film seems to be a compilation entirely of cum shots and we realise that Töst must have created it from his own back catalogue. As the girl's fist works on the phallus the camera closes in and the cock jerks and spurts and splashes onto the lens. As the semen trickles down, we see the girl, stifling a laugh, but winking into the camera, gradually come into focus.

At the end, we see the last of the girls climb into her bed;

Madame switches off the exterior neon sign and removes her chignon. Töst has been honest, clever and cruel. His heroines are complete people, his men disembodied nothings – at best slightly risible and sad. The movie isn't fair, but it has all the insight of a poacher turned gamekeeper, and perhaps of a man who grew up in a brothel.

The Absence of Real Desire, 1971, 35MM COLOUR (+8MM B/W), 90MINS

By this time, sex films in America were moving into their 'Hollywood', or as some might describe it 'fashionable', phase with decent budgets, good actors and coherent storylines. Trust Töst the pioneer to do something perverse. At one level, the film anticipates soft core popular American TV on the level of *Baywatch* and even *Sex and the City.* At another, he recalls the rather bleak and nihilistic perspective of *Fick Alles.* Töst cleverly mixed 35mm and 8mm formats for critical sequences.

His distributors were pleased with the success of *Super Bitch*, the irony of which escaped them. Apart from its faux-documentary disguise, they saw it as a sort of *Valley of the Dolls* meets *True Magazine.* They were therefore happy with whatever they saw of the outline of Töst's new project. This was titled *Girls with Time on Their Hands.* Equally evident is the debt *Debbie Does Dallas* owes to this movie. But if *Debbie* is jollier, it is much less well filmed and finished, and devoid of semiotic meaning.

As *Girls with Time* ,the film offers us a trio of Valley girls just out of college and bored silly. The title sequences fill in a necessary back-story of unsatisfactorily lost virginity, in cars to college kids and/or the local Hell's Angel. The girls are now mooching around somewhere in smart California. Töst as usual has reduced locations to virtually nothing and confines the action almost entirely to a classy and secluded suburban house with a pool.

We know from his star, Cayman Montrose, that he cast from a stable of wannabe actors, of whom California had a large supply. These girls were good-looking and happy with the idea of blue movies. It's likely too that they were from quite smart backgrounds. As Töst himself remarked when interviewed by *Midnight Blue*: 'Only well-educated girls can be both sexually incontinent and bored with sex at the same time. That's why they take drugs. Ordinary girls are just too honest.' On the men his only requirement – scrawled on the bottom of the shooting notes title page – was 'Lean, mean, must fuck well.'

From the beginning, Töst hits us with a dichotomy. He has split the screen and for three-quarters of it we are watching the bright, flat colours of a Hockney swimming pool, in the ripples of which shimmer the titles. But down in the bottom right quarter there is a grainy, old-style sex film and it is all briefs, legs, hair, slits, heavy swollen penises, grimacing mouths, fucking and the oozing of semen. These are the back stories of the girls' loss of innocence.

After this we are back with Hockney plus TV ad. California. Our girls alternately lie around drinking and popping pills, or are screwing anyone and everyone. There are implications of geographic movement in cars to clubs, the ocean and so forth. These were probably shot later by a second unit director. Töst himself tricked out the basement of the location to resemble a disco and a film studio for particular scenes.

The story, so far as it goes, simply traces the descent of our bored girls into complete sexual abandonment. For someone we know to be personally appreciative of and sympathetic to women, Töst is remarkably tough and cynical. Whilst he leaves us in no doubt that the men are just there for the sex, it is evident that so are the girls.

In his usual flat way, Töst builds the story in a series of accumulating paired scenarios. The sexual experience is followed by the evaluation, and leads to the escalation to the next level. The presumption is: neat sex but not ultimate pleasure.

The end is obvious, yet in Töst's unique way, a surprise. The girls are lucky to escape alive from a final, drug-fuelled gang-bang. Sperm-drenched, fucked in every orifice, they are almost senseless with satiety. They admit defeat. These scenes – and the whole movie – are highly sexually charged. Not least due to Töst's ability to motivate his female actors to be aroused and to come truly to orgasm. As one actress in it observed much later: 'Just going through the storyboard got me hot and bothered.' Coarse and brutal as the males are in the ultimate sex sequences, they are quite evidently responsive to what the women want. All these boys and girls got it on.

Then Töst does his thing. We slowly fade from the last glistening, leaking and swollen vulva, gaping anus, blank stare and bruised, semen-smeared mouth to the flat, bright swimming pool. Around it stand our heroines in bridal gowns, each with a handsome male in white tuxedo. Guests applaud. The girls look at each other. As ever, loath to move his camera, Töst gently shifts the focus so that the scene reduces into the distance. In the right-hand bottom corner we reprise each of the women's faces in grainy 8mm sex loop reality as they come to orgasm in the last and most extreme of their adventures.

The original release was under the title *Sunshine Girls* and without the 8mm inserts. It did well enough in America – especially on the West Coast – but did not get the big cable operators excited. Was it a simple business issue, or had Töst's unique vision baffled the gatekeepers of porn movie taste? Töst did a deal to gain East Coast and European rights. He re-titled it, kept the inserts and brought the film to continental Europe where it had considerable success, as it did in Japan, where Töst remains a well-regarded director in his field.

The Sick Room, 1975, 16mm Colour, 75mins

In the moral climate of today, this is a difficult film. It is Töst's last known work, in that whatever he filmed later he did anonymously and solely for the rent money. The reason it is difficult is that the theme is the seduction of a pubescent youth by an older woman. Not much older, to be sure, but on the face of it an under age kid and several school fellows are seduced by and subsequently sexually educated – even debauched – by not just one but two older females.

Töst's own background certainly gives him licence to deal with these matters and to take a sanguine view. On his own admission he lost his virginity at thirteen to an older woman. He has made it clear that the principal actor involved in this film was in fact eighteen. That may be legally exculpatory, but is not very helpful perceptually in 2006. Töst himself, shortly before his death, dismissed the whole thing. 'Everyone knows boys from puberty onward are dying to fuck. Protect whom you need to protect and leave the rest alone.'

That said, this is a very sexy, intimate and intense film reminiscent of Zola and his novel *Nana*. The context is a boarding school for boys. The situation is the arrival in the sick room of a patient. Töst's approach is perfectly suited to the claustrophobic nature of this story. Possibly his early life informed it. We never leave the sick room. It is plain and white with few furnishings other than six beds and small side tables like a dormitory.

The whole of the title sequence is one, long, black and white shot of the room with the credits rolling. The door opens, and a young man comes in and sits on the bed. There is a long pause – this is Töst, refusing to just get on with it as he toys with the sexual tension created by his knowledge of his audience expectation. The titles end and the film dissolves into colour. A strongly-built, though handsome, mature woman comes in. She takes a temperature, and commands the youth to stand and drop his trousers. She feels his balls. Nods, gestures and leaves. He begins to undress. We watch him become naked. He is maturely hung, though almost hairless. Then arrives the under-matron. She is pert, pretty, undeniably sexy, and she smiles at the youth's confusion.

Almost everything about the film has a silent movie quality. The set and clothes are all black, white and grey. Even skin tones are white. Only the eyes and genitals of the actors have real colour, which lends a startling vividness to the otherwise flat and almost dreamlike visual impression. As often with Töst, there is the sound not of dialogue as such but of people communicating and of things happening. Töst once said he got the idea from Jacques Tati's *Monsieur Hulot's Holiday*. In the sick room, over time, from the patient's perspective as he lies in the bed, we learn what he learns. The pretty under-matron and his perception of her face, smile, eyes, body; the moment when she discovers his erection; and his first experience of oral and other aspects of sex.

Subsequently, the head matron discovers them. Naked, the girl is forced to continue to fellate the youth whilst she is beaten. He, of course, comes and so does she. Since the matron has stripped herself to a basque and black stockings and has thrust a dildo into her vagina, this lacks real brutality, and has become a fantasy, indeed causing a dichotomy between arousal and laughter. The film continues to develop the relationship between sex and farce. As the youth lies in his bed, usually servicing or serviced by the under-matron, a whole procession of other boys and masters appears. The matron is a well-preserved and well-built female of her type; she enjoys a sound, practical S&M relationship with various masters. The under-matron meanwhile has a fine time with the boys, usually in twos and threes. She quite evidently enjoys the arousal of her patient's jealousy. He is placated by his being the only one she will fuck alone or allow to give her oral sex, but eventually he has to come to terms with her freedom. In one sequence she straddles his face as she sucks and masturbates a sequence of young men. We only see her back or her profile as our 'hero' gradually overcomes his jealousy, pushes her forward and begins to fuck her with angry intensity. It is clear that he has become excited by seeing her become more and more semen-drenched, as the viscous ejaculations drip from her mouth, breasts and hands.

The film concludes with a scene in which the sick room is full of people fucking. His initiator and lover is lying across him, penetrated fore and aft by masters and young men. She looks heavy-lidded at him and reaches for his penis, but he slides from the bed and walks naked from the room. Make of it what you will, Töst has teased us to the last about our desires and our pretensions.

This is an astonishingly erotic film, because of, not despite the humour. The boy's-eye-view is remarkable: possibly the best example of Töst's signature style. The camera only moves and focuses as would the boy – up, down, sideways, near here, over there. As *Screw* magazine wrote, 'If you want to know what it is like to be in bed and have a horny girl give you a blow job, have you suck her pussy or just get off on everyone else getting off, this shows you. And with enough jism to float a waterbed.'

Despite this accolade, *The Sick Room* did not achieve the success it should have. By this time, video was starting to replace film. The movie itself was too full-on for the erotica audience and too oddball for the porn fan. On the continent it achieved some distribution and later did better when transferred to video. In America it ran only in New York for a couple of months. It may be again that its limited success was not about the film, but about business issues. Töst no longer had powerful mentors.

Appendix 4
Social mores, semiotics and the behavioural zeitgeist as expressed in pornographic films

The following freelance article was intended for Rolling Stone *in 1998 but never published. The introduction is by Carrie King.*

I came to Bernd Töst's work late in the day. Töst had not produced a credited movie of merit since 1975. In fact, he had effectively left the film business in the late 1970s. I liked the man I met. Whilst as a feminist journalist I was hostile to the porn trade, and so very wary of his films, Töst struck me as having something to say. That something needed, in my view, to be said as the boundaries of what was permissible in sexual portrayal became blurred and the mendacity of Hollywood more apparent.

When we met, Töst was a rather sad, slightly shabby, and probably ill person. His long-time friend Dwight drove him to our meeting. I was struck by the affection evident between Töst and this big, tough African-American. Töst opened our conversation by asking that his fee, if any, went straight to Dwight. 'It's my rent,' he said. I had the impression that Töst was dependent on, if not actually living with, Dwight and his family at the time.

What follows is effectively an edited – but not embellished – transcript of what turned out to be a spontaneous Töst lecture. It never made print, which I regret and feel was a mistake.

This does not invalidate its worth or relevance today. I am glad for it to be published – albeit belatedly – in his biography.

'This title is really pretentious shit. I did not choose it. You or someone else wanted something egghead. I must admit that I may have helped. You can blame this on my European upbringing. A half-Danish, half-German boy brought up by a single mother in Paris and then war-time London who went to English public school and learned his craft in Soho can be expected to have some eccentricities. As our readers are intellectuals it may be a good plan to define our terms.

'If we want to simplify, the title might be "Customary behaviour, the use of symbols and what the influential people are up to".

'The pornographic film link is of course the focal point. It is a long time since I was in or indeed took very much notice of the business. But it is hard to avoid the presentation of sex in every aspect of our society's discourse. Whether this is good or bad or just natural is up to people out there to decide.

'I want to get rid of as many definition issues as possible. What most people would call a pornographic movie is one where actors' genitals are seen in sexual use. This simple criterion has been used to define pornography probably since men discovered crayons.

'There may be many possible extensions of meaning for specific groups. Violence of various kinds, degrees and contexts – whether sexual or combative – in movies has often been described as pornographic. Which leads to the other blurry boundary for pornography – the presence or absence of intellectual, moral or contextual content. The boundary is fuzzy, of course, because there is always the conflict between the prevailing general assumptions: how we see things – whoever we are – and where our influences lead us. That's true whether you are a dumb fuck or an intellectual.

'This article is not a history of censorship or sexual evolution. In truth I don't think we in the USA are much different from anyone else; or that societies have changed fundamentally over time. To look at representations of sexual activity has always been of interest to the people and a worry to authorities: the bounds of censorship alter through debate, legal ruling and experiment. Other countries operate a range of tolerances. I digress. Mores certainly change at the edges, and fashion history shows us how. We can also be sure that, whatever the apparent morality, real people were still doing something different. I make this point so I can get back to the present.

'Now, right now, the USA – old, young, born-again Christian and East Coast liberal fink – goes to bed with the image of their President with his cock in the mouth of a girl and then ejaculating onto her dress. How pornographic is this! For sure it is only verbally described and, of course, it's important news. Right now, zillions of people and dollars come together, to coin a phrase, to create the voyeuristic pleasure of watching cocks and cunts, guys and gals get it on in various ways and combinations. So, as a porn guy thinking of Monica, it is a commercial disaster that El Presidente's PR girl wasn't there with a camera.

'Social mores say all this is bad and sad. It is not something you would tell your mother. This is the mother who already knew what was under your mattress. What we do in our bedrooms, or wherever, is our business. The material we like to use to give us a buzz is also our choice. We are fortunate in the world that technology and market forces can show us and bring us what we want. Yet we still have shame. The mores still suggest that there is something illicit about sexual imagery. Oddly, there is more shame regarding our bodies than there is about our bodies' waste disposal functions. We are content to sit in a cubicle, or stand at a stall, and shit or piss in the company of strangers. We wouldn't, in general, dream of having sex in such circumstances. People do, of course, but this is not in the mores, even if it is in the zeitgeist.

'I would say too that our swearing is now both more liberal and yet still possessed of shame. To say "fuck," or to call someone a cunt or an asshole or a shit or whatever is not done in polite society, but is very commonplace and effectively legitimised. Yet the semiotics of these words take us back to Freud and our baby days when sex and excretion were muddied together – as possibly they still are. In that context, reflect on why it is that the excretory epithets are generally seen as less offensive than the genital ones.

'If the mores still insist on a decent dose of shame and guilt, the semiotics of style and beauty challenge us. The zeitgeist, as a driver of the symbols, is a bizarre mixture of hedonism and fear. While much of the world removes its clothing, Islam and fundamental Christianity have been keen to get muffled up. This is scary stuff in the zeitgeist where individualism and a good time are under threat. Terrorism, sexual disease and fat make *Vogue* seem very escapist.

'My point here is this. Way back in, say, the fifties, women in public, moral terms did not exist in a fleshly way between the bust and the knee. Women had big, pointy tits, and would lie demurely in your bedroom encased in elastic and bri-nylon if you gave them a fully-equipped kitchen. The customs, the symbols and the influences tied in because everything was controlled by the same people. Or rather, people with the same attitudes.

'Pornography was off the cultural map in general. Sex in any zeitgeist sense was heavily sanitised until we got to the Pill. Over the succeeding decades, women got freer and feistier, world economies expanded, pop music and TV showed the good times. It was all about being young and sexy and in charge of yourself. These things may be in the wrong order but they are all linked. In this discussion it is relevant that, whatever the mores were at mom and pop level, for the media and the people – who were no longer the same as your mom and dad – it was about girls and legs up to the ass and bare tits. Paglia won by a distance over Dworkin.

'In short, young women's bodies emerged, as they always do, as the key semiotic of the times. Some argue that the current semiotics are at root homosexual. The supposed gay grip of the fashion business is alleged to have created the thin, tight-buttocked, gamine look. Maybe that is so. Yet Coco Chanel did her bit as did all the designers of the 1920s. Tits and bums come and go. If we look at the iconography in fragrance or fashion, for a lot of the 1990s there was a lot of androgyny. Well, who knows? There was in the 1970s and in 1812. Pretty bodies can be rounded or angular. I could predict girls' bellies and groins as a new fashion. That's because they've got the confidence to open their legs and the semiotics now are all fuck me, fuck you. Some people might argue there's things there about fecundity or the supposed emasculation of men or our over-sexual, under-disciplined society. I neither know nor care.

'A couple of hundred years ago, artists – who have always wanted to paint naked people – had to use classical themes to achieve acceptance by the rich patrons who also wanted to look at them, but needed a pretext. You just have to look at Goya or Ingres to see that it was bums and groins then too, albeit plump ones. Later on, Picasso had fun ripping off some of Ingres' ideas and he put real cunts and pricks into the show. The mores say that's OK if they go in a gallery, and then the kids and the maiden aunt can see them. Just like it's OK to see someone's head being split open in a horror film but not... well, you think for yourselves what you can and cannot see, in what context, and decide.

'That said, the guardians of our mores are still worried. The symbols and the influence groups that drive them are taking us globally further on. We like lean, we want sexually voracious or confident and available women. They are slim, effective and in charge. Even in the routine porn film I have noticed that the girls are getting very assured and real with the camera and their colleagues. As in real life, the sex is on their terms in more cases.

'I would invite people to think about the interconnection between so-called soft porn, fashion and hard porn. As I said, nowadays the action is around the groin. Hips jut out and thighs are wide and taut. What are we all thinking when we look along the magazine rack – how nice the fabrics are? We may be, but the semiotics are about sex, and specifically, fucking.

'I think, as this piece of indulgence unfolds, I want to restate my belief in the essential honesty of pornography and the mendacity of other media. Let's reflect on why *Basic Instinct* remains famous. Just for a possible glimpse of an actor's cunt. Why has anal sex between heterosexuals achieved a degree of zeitgeist interest and discussion? Because of the success of the gay movement in promoting its lifestyle despite AIDS. Also, in my view, because fashion has declared big tits out and tight asses in. Also, because everyone in the whole world can see a cunt with a cock in it on every news-stand. So thirty years on from *Last Tango*, no porn film is without anal sex and, by the way, everyone knows now what gay men do and that they can do it too, and to girls. Is this consumer choice or what? And, of course, the digital camera and the webcam have deconstructed pornography and made post-modernists of us all. Anyone can now recreate their sexual behaviours and desires for themselves, or an audience. This is *Reader's Wives* in the internet age and everyone is equally sexy – or equally ordinary or equally and gloriously repellent. The professional is forced onto the margins. This may turn out well, if there is ever a market for quality films about sex in which it is worth paying to watch something exceptional. Failing that, there's nothing left but extreme sex and an audience of lazy voyeurs.

'Even in that weird country of my education, England, or Great Britain, or the UK – it always confused me – you can buy quite openly, albeit from a specialist and licensed shop, totally explicit videos and DVDs. So far as I can tell, these movies are vetted for content and you won't get anything the censors – society – regard as gross deviance. I don't know quite how it works everywhere, but the western consensus seems to proscribe, quite understandably and correctly in general terms: children, causes of real bodily harm and, I imagine, necrophiliac sequences and bestiality.

'Which leads me to my own problems with boundaries. If you are a true libertarian, you will have to reject censorship at every level. As a Marquis de Sade or whatever, you might want to elide sex, pain, coprophilia and, ultimately, death. There is a market for everything. Sex is a wild card and in that, the Bible was right about Adam and Eve and the snake, semiotically speaking. Different strokes for different folks, literally. So-called BDSM covers a very wide territory from the spice-up-your-sex-life pretend things to something really heavy. My censorship position is clear. If the sex involves real-time coercion and criminality then it isn't the showing that is wrong, it's the making.

'I am unhappy that the porn business – in which I have had some good times – suffers on occasion from exploitation of minors, poor people and so forth. I have to say though, so does the production of sport shoes, lingerie and whatever, and probably on a larger scale. Elsewhere I am on record as saying that I only filmed material my actors were comfortable with. If you don't see much rubber, bondage or violence in my films it is because of my own preferences. As a director, I am a voyeur too, but I am also a conduit for my audience. So I have filmed things that did not personally excite me. I have also filmed things I felt were potentially distasteful but which had legitimacy in the narrative, as in *Fick Alles*. I mean, how do you distinguish the semiotics of *Straw Dogs* or *Ai No Corrida* and *The Devil in Miss Jones*? My deal with producers was that I would only shoot what the crew was good with. It lost me work, but I can live with myself. I shot some garbage too, but I can say: at least the actors got off on what it seemed they got off on.

'The dilemma in the argument, for the people who control the zeitgeist, is about the impact of sexually explicit material on the weak-minded. The train of logic goes from the fantasy – that is, the untested reality – that, say, the rapist will offer as defence: "dressed like that she was asking for it", to the idea that pornographic films provoke these hideous and uncontrollable lusts. I don't know the answer. This is the ongoing debate.

'I shot fuck films. You have very little chance to be cute. My main work shows where I tried to take the thing. To the point, it is quite insane to suppose pornography fosters sexual deviance. I would say in this matter that there are no semiotics in porn any different from those operating in the rest of society's media of dialogue. Does a diet of porn desensitise more or less than violent video games or cheap newspapers? We porno people – even at our best – simplify existing fashion off the back of human sexual urges. I will venture one speculation on this topic. I believe there is a cultural difference between European-based pornography and that of America. In the USA we tend to do upbeat and cheerful. In Europe, they beat us on sleaze.

'As we are here in America, the USA, which I love, and we are with a fine intellectual journal, I would like to return to the title. It is mostly crap. Pornography is simply a generally benign outlet for inherent human instincts. Some – like sex – are flakier than others, it is judged. How pornography is manifested or categorised may or may not reflect the technology and cultural values of the time. The semiotics kind of go the same route. Everyone should read Henry Miller to understand real pants-down sex between men and women at the point of lust. Porno movies can be critiqued for suggesting that women just love to be screwed by several guys and ejaculated over. They can also be charged with suggesting that men should have big dicks in a permanent state of erection. Please, good people, don't worry so much. It is all in the head. Those nice men and ladies only propose to you that a good fuck is fun, so be glad and enjoy your fantasies. It's better than, say, watching folk shoot each other.

'That said, the semiotics of sex are an interesting bellwether of social conditions. Our society is somehow in confrontation between the liberal and the constrained. I've been reading about the Roman Empire in the years when it moved from republic to dictatorial rule. I believe we are pretty much where they were. We have dominant lawyers, generals, business fat cats, corrupt and supine politicians and a population of greedy, overfed plebeians and dispossessed immigrants. Overseas our empire of commerce and influence is a restive and increasingly resentful populace of wannabes held in check by money, a few loyal allies and our military might. The sex business is in overdrive. Film, fashion, music; babies, it is all sex, drugs and rock 'n' roll. Out there in the boondocks, some frightening forces gather to challenge us all. There are many things they hate about our society; women and sex are just part of it. It won't be porno that brings us down, but the cynicism of our businesses, the opportunism of our politicians and the fanaticism of the religious and intolerant in society. Watch out, America, watch out, world; the future is coming to fuck you and you won't like it. Compared to, say, one of my movies.'

Appendix 5
Bernd Töst and Edna Weiskopf in debate

The following edited transcript is taken from a video-recorded debate between Töst and Edna Weiskopf (a leading radical feminist of the decade) in 1979. The interview had been taped for the British TV programme *Arena* but was never broadcast. The interviewer simply introduces the two, billing Töst as 'a noted pornographic filmmaker' and Weiskopf as 'a feminist who makes Andrea Dworkin and Gloria Steinem look like tarts'.

EW: I want to say that is offensive. My sisters are my fellow warriors in the cause of toppling male domination.
BT: I'm with you on that. Did you see *Super Bitch*?
EW: Are you bullshitting me?
BT: No, I am absolutely for equal rights.
EW: So why are you an oppressor of women?
BT: I am not.
EW: You are a pornographer and that is a leading part of the male system of slavery.
BT: Why exactly?
EW: Because you make money out of showing women being sexually abused.
BT: That is factually incorrect. I make a barely adequate living out of showing people fucking each other. The audience and the exploitation

is small compared to the fashion business run by women.

EW: By men. It is the same. Women are used, humiliated and exploited. You all feed male fantasies of aggression.

BT: Why don't you define your terms for me – and for the viewers.

EW: How do I begin from the millennia in which women have been used as breed stock, sexual toys and the despised possessions of men?

BT: That bit I concede for the most part. But times get better and whilst there is a way to go I don't see how this involves my movies.

EW: Because they continue the themes of oppression, objectivisation and exploitation.

BT: Well, Edna, if I can call you that, not in my movies they don't. I'll grant you some pornography does that, but so do most religions. Most pornography is just about people fucking each other or playing sexual games. It's fantasy, babe, based on what we all do.

EW: Fantasy for men to masturbate over.

BT: Well, men do that, you know. You girls aren't always in the mood.

EW: That is the whole point. Women are just receptacles for men to stick their disgusting organs into.

BT: So Edna, how disgusting is a cock compared to a cunt?

EW: You are offensive.

BT: No, Ms Weiskopf, you are offensive. Just why

is a penis more offensive than a vagina and why is it disgusting for men and women to have sexual intercourse?

EW: I am not talking of the organs – though your phrasing shows you up – but of the attitude. To adopt your language: men fuck, women are fucked. It is a classic victim and oppressor relationship, which has carried through from its original biological imperative of penetration to its modern socio-economic bondage of conquest.

BT: I think I've agreed the case for female equality. I don't know what to do about the biology – Charles Darwin maybe should have told us. Or maybe, since science has advanced, you ladies can go with artificial insemination. Which means my films will help the guys jack off for you. Or maybe the idea of pleasure isn't in your idea of procreation. That said, as a simple moviemaker, I am struggling with your thesis about my business and the abuse of women. I always had the naïve idea that people like to see people fucking and my actors were happy to fuck each other on camera and we all went home feeling good.

EW: How can you say this when your films show women being abused, penetrated, masturbated over, beaten? Your films are about rape.

BT: Have you seen my films?

EW: Yes. I made sure to watch them all before this programme.

BT: Well, thank you for that. To be candid, I am not sure if I am now defending my own work or

that of an entire industry.
EW: It makes no difference to me.
BT: OK, then let's just say this is me talking about my work and it's about what I believe.

(There is a break here and whilst the tape is still on we hear Bernd say to someone, 'Jesus, this bitch is one tedious lady. I'm getting bored, kids, this is a no-win thing.')

EW: I don't care what you say, men dominate our social, economic and political agenda. You import prostitutes from poor nations, you mutilate our genitals and you deny us birth control. Even where we have the vote we get less pay and we still have to submit to men because we have no choice. Worse, because our bodies have economic value they are therefore made the commercial icons of male lust. If females find it acceptable to sell their sexuality for money it is their sad submission. As victims, weaker sisters maybe have to select that option.
BT: You know, I am a simple man. I respect and like women, I loved my mother. I get upset when I read about women being abused. In my business we have human beings of both sexes who have the physical and mental skill and the inclination to create sexually explicit ideas on camera. They volunteer, they are paid well – especially the women, by the way – and they have stuff like medical care. No one does what they don't

want. Most often they have fun, and for me that's essential. I will concede that in some sectors of the sex business things are bad, and that's regrettable, but not universal.

EW: That may be. You are still in the business of the portrayal of women as sexual objects.

BT: No, I'm in the business of showing sex as a central thing we do and fantasise about doing well and want to watch. My assumption personally is that women have strong sex drives too. We men may satisfy them badly but we have the dicks and you have the cunts. As Camilla Paglia once said, 'Men get it up, women deal with it.' To leave aside the global issues, how we get it together is another matter. My films have unfailingly assigned personal choice in storyline roles and specific activities to my actors. I have also always asked questions about the audience's attitudes and made it harder to get your rocks off on glib images. *Fick Alles* was certainly about the issues of women's use of and control over their bodies. I would have thought you would approve at least that she shot the rapists. I share things with my actors. In fairness to my industry colleagues, I believe that, whatever the artistic view, anyone worth knowing will respect the team.

EW: You are like a Roman Emperor who says that his gladiators are well-treated.

BT: If you say so. In my case, I am not an Emperor and my gladiators are volunteers.

(There is a rustle of microphones and we hear '...fucking BBC' from EW and 'Get me a cab back to Soho...' from Töst.)

Appendix 6
Extract transcript of proceedings of the Grand Jury, in the State of California, in the matter of The People versus Rumer Tissick

District Attorney (DA): You are Bernard Tōst, French citizen and resident alien in the State of California?
Bernd Tōst (BT): Bernd Tōst for the record – the rest is fine.
DA: Mr Tōst, were you employed by Hollywood Personal Services Inc. between 1987 and 1991?
BT: Yes.
DA: Will you please describe your role to the jury?
BT: I was hired to assist my employer's clients to make home videos.
DA: Were these videos of a sexual nature?
BT: They were.
DA: Would you describe them as graphic and explicit?
BT: I would say so.
DA: Did they involve several people, unclothed, engaged in coition and deviant acts of oral and other forms of congress between unmarried persons?
BT: Oftentimes they did. At others they just involved maybe two people, like a husband and his wife, or girlfriend.

DA: What was the most common form of activity you were asked to assist in filming?
BT: Well, it's hard to say. It was just people having sex in various ways.
DA: Why did people request your services?
BT: The film thing? Oh well, it's a human characteristic. We're a watching, sentient and recording species. Many people like to keep the record.
DA: There was no sense of a hidden agenda – blackmail, for example?
BT: Not where I was. The job was just to set it up, make it look good and hand it over.
DA: Perhaps, Mr Töst, you could take a few moments to describe the sort of assignments you were sent on.
BT: Sure. One sort was when, say, a couple wanted a record of themselves. I'd go along and set up the camera, or maybe two, for them and then take the tapes away and process them – editing and so on. On occasion, I'd be asked to stay and do the filming myself. Some people don't mind being watched, or they actively like it; it depends.
The other sort was when it was kind of a party, you understand. I could do the filming, but quite often they wanted it done covertly, you know. So I'd set up several cameras in rooms or in bushes near the pool, or behind one-way mirrors. They'd just run for a set period of time – a few hours. All I had to do was collect and edit them.
DA: At these parties, were you in attendance all

the time?
BT: Often, though not always. I mean, I had to keep an eye on the cameras and tapes and so forth. People wanted a professional product.
DA: So in every case you were in a good position to observe what went on?
BT: I guess so, up to a point.
DA: Up to what point?
BT: Well, I couldn't be everywhere; the cameras had a specific range of view and there were rooms where we didn't operate like the bathrooms. Except occasionally.
DA: You'll be aware, Mr Töst, of the charges facing the defendant?
BT: Of course.
DA: At any time in your employment did Mr Tissick discuss the supply of participants, drugs or the type of activity to be undertaken?
BT: Absolutely not.
DA: Didn't you find that odd?
BT: No. I was a $200 a day technician paid to provide very rich people with a movie record of their amusements. They provided the location, the guests, their refreshments and anything else they needed. I was about as visible as the second footman.
DA: In being so invisible and with a video recorder, you were in a good position to notice a great deal.
BT: As I said before, up to a point.
DA: Did you notice any females who looked under age, did you see drugs being solicited or offered,

did you observe any obscene acts such as sodomy being performed?

BT: Well, sir, apart from ladies who were self-evidently on the other side of mature, I saw no females without well-developed tits and a full bush of pubic hair. Except for those, of course, who shaved that area. But my estimation was that they were all qualified to buy a gentleman a drink in a bar. I have to say, there were recreational drugs other than alcohol being consumed, but so far as I recall, they all seemed to be personal or communal property. I had no idea sodomy was still illegal. Put it this way, whatever went on at these events seemed to me to be consensual and conducted between people who were invited and knew each other and wanted to play.

DA: I hope you are not being flippant, Mr Töst.

BT: No, sir. I am trying to be clear and accurate.

DA: Is it true you earn a living making pornographic films?

BT: I used to. I would call them films about sex.

DA: Whatever. It makes you an expert in the subject, I imagine?

BT: Sure, but there are hundreds of others.

DA: That is, regrettably, quite probable. My point is simply that you are in a position to know whether or not the protagonists in these events were, if you will, private citizens or paid sexual partners?

BT: Normally I would go along with that. In this town it's more difficult. Half the young females in

LA have aspirations to get into showbusiness. To be candid, quite a number of those will try to get there on whatever couch seems most promising. You don't need to offer these girls money. An invitation to a party where there are real film people will do. The truth is, everywhere in the world are pretty young girls who are making choices. They want to have a good life and they will decide if they are going to marry it, use their brains for it, or just open their legs. Feminists get het up because many, if not most women, do all three.

DA: Thank you for your observations. I am sure many honourable American women will be gratified to hear your estimation of their virtue. Does your answer imply therefore that in your evidently informed, if sadly jaundiced, opinion, young girls were present at these events, suborned as sexual toys by the promise of work in the film industry?

BT: You'll have to ask the hosts and the guests that question. It isn't for me to assume their motives.

DA: Mr Töst, you are not represented by legal counsel.

BT: No. I couldn't afford the fee and in any case I have nothing to hide.

DA: Have you been approached by any third parties regarding your testimony?

BT: Absolutely not. Unless you count *Confidential* magazine, who wanted a story.

DA: And?

BT: I had nothing to tell them and nothing to sell them.
DA: Thank you, Mr Töst. Please do not leave California until the hearing is terminated.

The hearing terminated two weeks later and Töst left for New York. He did not return to California for some while.